Hunt for the Last Cat

Hunt for the Last Cat

Justin Denzel

Philomel Books
New York

To Jo,
Just for Being There

Copyright © 1991 by Justin Denzel.
All rights reserved. This book, or parts thereof,
may not be reproduced in any form without
permission in writing from the publisher.
Philomel Books, a division of
The Putnam & Grosset Book Group
200 Madison Avenue, New York, NY 10016.
Published simultaneously in Canada.
Book design by Jean Weiss.
The text is set in Aster.

Library of Congress Cataloging-in-Publication Data
　　Denzel, Justin F.
　　Hunt for the last cat : a novel / by Justin Denzel.
　　p.　cm.
　　Summary: Twelve-year-old Thorn feels conflicting loyalties when
　　members of his clan blame his friend Fonn, a girl from a rival clan,
　　for the marauding actions of a man-eating sabertooth cat.
　　ISBN 0-399-22101-8
　　[1. Man, Prehistoric—Fiction.　2. Saber-toothed tigers—Fiction.]
　　I. Title. PZ7.D4377Hu　1991
　　[Fic]—dc20　91-11537　CIP　AC
　　First Impression
　　10 9 8 7 6 5 4 3 2 1

ACKNOWLEDGMENTS ·

My sincere thanks to go the intrepid explorers, anthropologists and other scientists who dove deep into the many sinkholes of Florida to bring up the bones of Paleo-Indians, sabertooth cats and giant sloths; to the persistent diggers who braved the choking dust of open phosphate beds to unearth the remains of mastodons, mammoths and other ancient beasts; and not least to the archaeologists and collectors who followed the trail of Clovis spearheads across the country and down the length of the Florida peninsula, from Tallahassee to Key West. By their long and patient efforts a record of prehistoric Florida was brought to light, a record upon which this story is based.

I express my gratitude also to Patricia Lee Gauch and her helpful staff at Philomel Books. They checked the manuscript innumerable times, and

· 6

their professional criticism and astute advice improved the story immensely.

Finally, I acknowledge my debt to the Harry A. Sprague Library at Montclair State College in Upper Montclair, New Jersey. Over the years, its collection of scientific periodicals, textbooks and journals has been a valuable source of information, and its friendly staff always courteous and helpful.

PROLOGUE ·

Eight thousand years ago the age of the giant mammals was coming to an end: mammoths and mastodons, longhorn bison, ground sloths were dying out across the world. For a while some of the giants lingered on in the subtropical lands of what is now Florida. There, a few Paleo-Indians lived among them. Compared with the animals, they were puny and vulnerable. But they could think, and plan, and look ahead, and that gave them an edge over the giant beasts.

This is the story of a Paleo-Indian boy and girl and their adventures in that primitive land facing one of the last of the great Sabertooth tigers. It is fiction, but it is based on the latest findings of science and prehistory. It could have happened.

ONE ·

THE MOON WAS STILL HIGH when Smilodon, the big sabertooth cat, came up out of the canebrake and
stalked through the stand of dahoon trees. He padded along slowly, head down, sniffing the damp
earth. For almost five days now he had gone without
food, while the burning festering slash wound in his
thigh stiffened his springing muscles and denied him
the chance for a quick, easy kill. Silently he prowled
along the riverbank, looking for an unwary tapir or
a dozing river hog, anything that would help ease
the gnawing sensation in his empty stomach. Yet
after hunting all day he found nothing.

He padded on, his large amber eyes searching every shadow, his twitching ears picking up every
sound. From time to time he stopped and lowered
his head. He braced himself, took in a deep breath
and roared, churning up dust and leaves from the
ground in front of him. The heavy sound rumbled

like thunder far into the night, but it evoked no response, for there was no mate to hear his call, no rival sabertooth male to answer his challenge.

The cat was huge, with gleaming white fangs protruding from his upper jaw. He was long and lean, and powerful shoulder muscles rippled under his tawny hide. But he was old now, perhaps thirteen summers, and he had come north, driven out of his territory by a younger, stronger male, to prowl alone in this new land.

Thorn, the Paleo-Indian boy, waded waist-deep in water as a pale moon traced a golden path across the river. A flaming reed torch, propped between two corkwood logs, floated near his elbow and cast an eerie glow around him. With his fishing spear held high, he stared into the depths, searching for the dark shadow of a passing bowfin or garfish attracted to the light.

Tree frogs filled the night with their strident chorus. Restless parakeets, roosting in the overhanging branches of the dahoon trees, chattered and squawked. Somewhere in the darkness a bull alligator bellowed.

Thorn was tall for his age, with skin the color of new mahogany. The moonlight glistened off his long black hair and shadowed the curves of his high cheekbones. His young face was boyishly handsome, and there was a look of wildness in his dark eyes.

He waited patiently, feeling the warm current lapping against his thighs. Suddenly he thrust his spear into the water. It shivered and twisted as if it were alive, and he pulled it up with a dripping garfish squirming between the bony prongs.

The boy smiled as he took the fish from the end of the spear. He strung a length of pigeon vine through the fish's gills and slung it across his back with the five others he had already caught. He leaned over the water again, masking the rippling reflections with his left hand, holding his spear ready in the other.

He watched patiently, yet nothing came. While he waited he wondered what it must be like to be a fish. He pulled the floating torch closer, took a deep breath and plunged his head under the water. When he opened his eyes he could see the flickering light skip across the sandy bottom. Still holding his breath, he looked around and pretended he was a savage garfish looking for a frog. Small schools of minnows darted here and there beneath his eyes. A half-grown catfish wiggled between his legs, a soft-shell turtle plodded across the sandy floor. When he was out of breath he lifted his head and gasped for air. It became a game, and he tried it again and again and for a little while forgot why he was there.

Once more he put his face under the water and watched the dancing reflections of the torchlight playing across the sandy floor of the river. This time he saw a dark, shadowy form snaking its way along the bottom. With undulating curves, the creature swam toward him. The boy lifted his head slowly and shook the drops from his eyes. Then he stared back into the depths, grinning. "It has been a long time since we have had eel," he said half aloud. "Now, if I am lucky, Nema will be pleased."

He braced himself and waited for the right moment. He knew it would not be easy. The shimmering reflections of the water and the moving shadows could spoil his aim.

The eel came on in winding curves, smoothly, slowly. It was almost as long as his spear and as thick as his forearm. "Come, snakefish," he said under his breath. "Come closer, closer, a little closer." He raised his arm high. His body tensed as the long, dark shadow passed beneath him. With a powerful thrust he plunged his spear deep into the water.

He felt the weapon shudder. Instantly it was pulled out of his hand and was swept upstream, twisting, swinging back and forth as it bobbed against the current. Thorn leaped after it, splashing headlong through the water. He reached out and grasped it just as it was about to get away. He pulled and tugged, and finally lifted it out of the water.

The big snakelike fish was caught firmly between the prongs of the spear. Its thick black body glistened in the torchlight. As it wriggled and squirmed, its wet tail slapped Thorn across the face and chest. The boy reached up to grab it behind the head. But he was not quick enough: the fish turned and bit him savagely on the hand.

He struggled with the fish as he took it out of the prongs and held it tight. But the fish was slimy. Thorn felt it slipping out of his grasp. It is easier to hold an angry rattlesnake, he thought. He ran to shore, dropped his spear to the ground, and picked up a handful of dry sand and rubbed it over the eel's body.

"You are the biggest snakefish I have ever seen," he said. "You fight like a demon, but now my grip is strong and you cannot get away."

Once again the fish squirmed. It got its head free. It snapped and turned and bit him painfully on the finger. The boy winced. "Ouch! You would eat me if you could, but soon I will eat you." Thorn took his flint knife from his belt and stabbed the fish through the head, holding it until its struggle ended. Then he passed a length of vine through its gills and mouth and tied it securely to the other fish hanging over his shoulder. With that done he went back into the water and speared two more garfish and a big bowfin.

Satisfied with the night's catch, Thorn started to wade ashore. He had only taken a few steps when a girl's voice rang out, "Look out—behind you."

Thorn turned quickly to see an alligator swimming toward him, its eyes sparkling like twin rubies in the light of his torch. It came on silently, gliding across the dark water. Judging by the distance between its eyes, Thorn knew it was a big one. He waited until the beast was almost upon him. Then he lashed out at it and struck it across the snout with the blunt end of his fishing spear. There was a splash and a swirl of water as the alligator slipped away and disappeared into the black depths.

Thorn glanced toward the riverbank where the girl was standing. Moonlight played off her long dark hair and a tame fish crow sat on her shoulder clicking its bill, calling *ca-ha, ca-ha*.

The boy waded ashore with his heavy string of fish. By the time he reached the bank, the girl was gone. He shook his head, disappointed. He would have liked to talk with her. She is a ghost, he thought, she disappears like the mist on the river.

He glanced up and down the bank, peering into the darkness. He saw no movement. He heard nothing but the tree frogs and the chattering parakeets. Then he looked down, and in the light of the moon he saw the blood of the freshly killed fish dripping on the back of his legs. Now he knew why the big alligator had attacked. He felt a blush of shame, for even a clan boy should know that blood in the water is tempting bait.

He was sure the girl would know about that. She had come not long ago, mysteriously, from the west. He had seen her twice before but only for fleeting moments.

She was shy and she moved like a shadow. But this much he knew: her name was Fonn. Nema said she was the daughter of Mogon, a great hunter from the land of the Lake Dwellers, where the bad sickness had been. Mostly she walked alone. The clan people called her "the spirit girl." They said she talked to the animals and was a friend of Great Claw, the shaggy old ground sloth. The hunters said she ran with the llamas, and once Thorn had seen her walking beside the mastodons, close to Long Tusk. Because of this, many clan people thought she must be a ghost spirit.

Thorn was not sure. She did not seem like a spirit. Yet in truth he did not know what a spirit should look like. He knew she often followed him, and it made him uneasy. Why did she not come out of the shadows and talk? Maybe because she feared the clan people. Twice they had chased her away. Now she was afraid, afraid of what they might do if they caught her. Or maybe she thought he was only a child and of no concern. He shrugged. I am twelve summers and I hunt and fish like a man. Even Oom says so, and he is the one who taught me. He should know.

Thorn picked up his spear and his torch. A small bundle of sassafras twigs lay on the bank where he had left them. He gathered them up, tucked them under his belt and made his way along the river. He stepped silently across the damp sand, listening to the howl of a dire wolf in the distance. He could still hear the girl's fish crow calling *ca-ha, ca-ha,* and he knew she was not far away.

Holding his torch high, he followed the bend of the river. He was weighed down by the fish slung across his shoulder. The river was good tonight, he thought. Nema will be happy. I will give her the eel and the bowfin. Two of the garfish will be for the shaman. The rest I will give to Oom.

As he strolled along in the moonlight he smiled in anticipation. I will tell Oom all about the fight with the eel. Maybe I will tell him how the spirit girl warned me of the alligator. His smile broadened. But I think he will laugh and say I am making stories again. The good thoughts made Thorn hurry on, following the trail beside the riverbank. A warm breeze touched his face and he heard the water lapping against the bowlike knees of the cypress trees across the river.

Then, all at once, a vibrant roar filled the night. It came from upstream, a long, heavy, deep-throated sound that shattered the darkness. The tree frogs ceased their calling, the wolf was quiet.

Thorn waited, listening, his eyes wide, staring into the darkness. A jaguar? he thought. Maybe a big one. Yet the sound was strange. It was deeper, more powerful than a jaguar.

The boy started walking again, quietly, glancing back over his shoulder in the darkness, following the sandy bank of the stream. Just ahead of him a tapir splashed into the river, and he heard the shrill cry of a crested eagle.

Farther on he smelled the pungent odor of cat, strong and overpowering. He shook his head to drive the odor from his nostrils. This smell is different, he thought. He took a few more steps.

Then he saw the footprint. He stopped abruptly and thrust his torch upright into the soft earth. He dropped the string of fish on the ground. Falling to his knees, he spread out the fingers of his hands and placed them in the damp pug mark. They fit easily with room to spare. Thorn cringed. "Twice as big as a jaguar," he said, half aloud. "I must tell Oom. He will know what it is."

Suddenly he heard a sound behind him. The palmetto bushes parted as if in a soft wind. Thorn spun around. He had only his slender fish spear and his flint knife. He picked up the torch and thrust it out in front of him. In its flickering light he saw a slender, shadowy form. It was the spirit girl. She had come like a wild creature out of the night, her dark eyes reflecting the moonlight. She stood a few steps away and held her finger to her lips in a gesture of silence.

Thorn saw her high cheekbones, much like his own, and her gently rounded face. He waited, his heart pounding from the sudden fright.

She spoke in a hushed voice as if announcing a secret. "Tell the clan people to set fires around the camp and stay in their huts tonight."

"Because of the roar?" asked Thorn.

"Yes," said Fonn. "A new beast walks the forest."

Thorn pointed at the track in the damp earth. "Then he is larger than a jaguar."

"It is the mark of Smilodon," the girl said.

The boy sucked in his breath. His eyes grew wide. "He is back? You have seen him?"

"No," said Fonn, "but I know he comes from beyond the swamps. I can smell the path he walks. My crow tells me where he goes."

"It has been nearly four summers," said Thorn. He glanced around in the darkness. "Now the evil cat is back, just as the shaman said."

The girl shook her head and threw her long dark hair back over her shoulders. "The cat is neither good nor evil. He is an old sabertooth. He searches for food and new land in which to hunt."

For a moment Thorn's lips pressed tight. Then he said, "It is a ghost—the ghost of the cat that killed my father."

"No," said the girl. "This beast is flesh and blood, as real as you and I."

"How can that be? Oom killed Smilodon nearly four summers ago."

"There are other Smilodons," said the girl. "Not as many, but there are some. When one dies another comes to take its place."

Thorn glanced at the girl and shook his head. "Our shaman will say it is a ghost. He has seen the sign many times in his sleep, and he says that one day the spirit of Smilodon will come back to take revenge."

"Hear me, clan boy," said Fonn, stepping closer. "This beast is real—an old rogue. Here he will find no mate, and few large beasts on which to feed."

"How do you know?"

"Because the roar went far through the night. There was no answer. This cat hunts alone, without help. Because of this he will often go hungry."

Thorn frowned. "Then the clan people will live in fear again."

"Yes," said Fonn. "It will take many brave hunters to kill this one."

Thorn threw back his shoulders. "Then I will kill Smilodon, as he killed my father." He saw the flicker of a smile on the girl's lips and he knew she thought he was strutting like a wood pigeon.

"You speak bravely, clan boy. But it will take more than one strong arm. And it will take many spears."

Thorn heard her speak, but his mind was already racing ahead. There must be a way, he thought. A trap, a snare, a pitfall—that was it, he would use a pitfall.

He stood there watching the girl in the moonlight. He could not see her clearly, yet he sensed she was not much older than he was, maybe fourteen or fifteen summers. And he knew she was swift, for she had been seen running with the longhorn bison. Then he asked the questions that were on the tip of his tongue: "Why do you walk alone? Why do you not hunt with your clan?"

The girl winced. "Someday I will tell you. Now there is no time. You must go quickly and warn your people."

"And you?" asked Thorn.

"I will sleep high in the branches of the oak wood, where Smilodon cannot climb." She turned quickly toward a stand of palmetto bushes. "Now go, before the cat picks up your scent." As she disappeared into the shadows the boy heard her hushed voice once again. "Smilodon is no ghost."

·TWO

AS THORN MADE HIS WAY through the dark forest he felt uneasy. He heard a crackling sound in the willow bushes behind him. He stopped and glanced back over his shoulder. Then he turned up through the loblolly pines, running, watching his shadow chase along beside him. His bare feet padded soundlessly over the ground cover of pine needles, his shoulders hunched under the burden of fish.

Ever since he was a child he had heard stories about the great beast, Smilodon, a huge tawny cat that prowled the forests of the clan people, sometimes coming close to camp. It was larger than the biggest jaguar, strong and powerful, with fangs as long as spearheads protruding from its upper jaw. Thorn had never seen it alive. But every day he saw it in death, for even now the huge tan pelt of the one Oom had killed covered the floor of Nema's hut.

The elders spoke of Smilodon in whispers. It was

an evil demon that came in the night and dragged
the clan people out of their beds and devoured them.
They told of its enormous size, its haunting yellow
eyes and savage disposition. Mostly it preyed on
mastodon calves and the young of giant ground
sloths. But when driven by hunger, it would stalk
the clan people as they hunted or fished along the
riverbanks or dug for roots in the fields. The jaguar
could be frightened off and the puma lived in the
shadows—but Smilodon prowled without fear, lord
of the forest and grasslands.

Just above a gentle rise, Thorn reached the clearing near the edge of the flatwoods where a group of
nine palm-thatched huts crowded in an erratic circle. They were flimsy dwellings constructed of bent
poles over which were lashed hides, strips of bark,
grass matting and palmetto fronds. Low, domelike
structures, they were built as protection against the
tropical sun and as shelter from the heavy rains.

Tall groves of cabbage palms and scattered stands
of bumelia bushes grew on the opposite side of the
little camp, facing the open grasslands.

Thorn made his way to a hut near the edge of the
camp where a dim light flickered between cracks in
the thatch. He hunched down and pushed his way
through the palm-leaf opening.

The odor of sassafras tea filled his nostrils. The
sweet smell came from a skin sack boiling and bub-
bling over a small hearth fire in the center of the
room. The floor was hard-packed sand, and a large
tawny hide covered the back half of the hut.

An old woman sat on the edge of the pelt with her legs tucked up beneath her. She bent over as she cut papaw fruit with a flint knife and mashed the soft yellow pulp on a flat stone. Her face was round with dark slanting eyes and fat cheeks. Perspiration beaded her face, and licks of gray hair were plastered against her damp forehead. Her flat nose twitched as she chewed on a short sprig of sassafras.

She glanced up quickly and frowned, moving the twig across her lips to the opposite corner of her mouth. "It is late," she said. "I worry."

Thorn laid his fishing spear on the ground. He removed the small bundle of twigs from his belt and held it out to her. "They are from the tips of the new ague trees down by the river," he said.

The old woman grinned. She spat out the twig she was chewing on and replaced it with a new one. She nibbled on the end of it for a moment. "Humm," she said, "fresh and sweet." Then she scowled up at him, pretending to be angry. "You are still late."

"The fishing was good?" said Thorn.

She smiled, nodding her head. "And you play again."

Thorn picked up his fish spear and placed it at the back of the hut. "Nema, I think you see through the trees."

"What I see is your wet hair," she said, chuckling. "There is no rain. Maybe you swim after your fish."

Thorn smiled back at her. He thought to tell her about the alligator. Then he changed his mind and said nothing. He would tell her about Smilodon later.

"How many did you get?" she asked.

"Eight gars, and a bowfin and a snakefish," said Thorn.

When the woman saw the dangling eel her eyes lit up. She opened her mouth in a toothless grin. "You are a good fisherman. Tomorrow we eat well."

Thorn smiled. Nema would cut the eel into sections and seep it in the juice of swamp onions. Afterward she would bake it slowly over hot embers until it was crisp and tasty. This they would eat along with arrowroot and wild potato and a bread made of bulrush flour. Thorn was sure that only Nema could make such a meal.

For as long as he could remember he had lived with this woman, Nema, the mother of his father. His own mother had died when he was not yet three summers. It seemed such a long time ago.

He thought of the news he had to tell, and sat down beside Nema and looked into her dark brown face. It was a face full of wrinkles and lines. The lines showed memories of more than forty summers passed. Her hearing was not always good, and Thorn reached out gently, took her chin in his hand and turned her head so that she looked at him. He smelled the spicy odor of the twig she was chewing. Only when she slept was she without her sassafras or ague twig, and Thorn brought her fresh ones almost every day.

Now he looked into her dark eyes, wondering how to tell her the bad news. "Nema," he said in a calm voice, trying not to frighten her, "did you hear the roar?"

The woman shook her head, her eyes blank. "No, I heard nothing," she said. She reached up and put her hand on his arm and smiled. "I think maybe you have a story to tell."

"No, Nema, not this time." Thorn hesitated. Then he looked directly into her face. He spoke slowly and deliberately. "Smilodon is back."

For a moment the woman's expression didn't change. Then she laughed and slapped him roughly on the shoulder. "Bah," she said, "you have no story tonight, so you make one up."

"Nema, I tell the truth. Even now the evil cat prowls the forest near the camp."

Her eyes grew wide. "You saw him?"

"No, I heard his roar and I saw his track down by the river."

Nema shook her head, still unwilling to believe. "Ach, the jaguar roars, the puma leaves a track. How do you know it is Smilodon?"

"I am sure," said Thorn. He held up his two hands and made a large circle with his fingers. "His mark was larger than that." He was silent for a moment. Then he went on. "Even the spirit girl says it is so."

Nema looked up quickly. "The spirit girl? You spoke with her?"

"Down by the river—this very night."

"It is not good," said Nema. Shadows danced on the thatched wall behind her. "The spirit girl would know. A sabertooth cat needs much food, but most of the giant beasts are gone. Great Claw is the last of the ground sloths. The mastodons and mammoths are few. Even the great cave bears are no more. Why this should be, I do not know. Maybe a sickness is driving them away." She held up her hands in a sweeping gesture of confusion. "The land is changing. When my father was a boy the giant beasts were many. Now there are few. Today the grasslands run with the smaller animals; many bison, the forests are filled with deer. But they are swift. Smilodon cannot catch them." She looked up at Thorn. "If he goes hungry he will turn on the people."

"Maybe this one is a ghost—it will not need to eat," Thorn said. "Yet the spirit girl says it is real." He shook his head. "I do not know."

"Nor do I," said Nema. "I only know that Dour has seen the sign many times in his sleep and in the ashes of the bay leaves. If Dour is right, then the spirits are angry. The cat may come here." She brushed her hand over the soft fur of the pelt. "For I am the one who cut off his skin. I am the one who scraped out his skull."

Thorn jumped up. "No, Nema, do not say that." He reached down and took her hands in his, and squeezed them with all his might. "I will not let him come, Nema. I will kill him, just as he killed my father. There must be a way. Oom will help me."

Nema took her hands out of his and squeezed his wrists lightly. "Let us hope the spirit girl is right," she said. "If Smilodon is no ghost, maybe he will wander away."

Thorn was not sure about this. He stood upright in the center of the hut, his head almost touching the low roof. He turned and picked up a handful of reeds from a small pile near the back of the hut. He bound them together with a string of plant fiber and dipped one end into a large shell of fish oil. Then he lit this end from the fire, and picked up the string of garfish and the bowfin. "I will bring fish to the shaman," he said. "Then I will see Oom."

Nema sighed. "Yes," she said, "Oom will help. But Dour will call up the spirits, and the answer will be bad. When your father lived the spirits were good."

As he turned to go, the boy looked back and saw the worry on the old woman's face.

THREE ·

MOONLIGHT FILTERED THROUGH the branches of the swaying cabbage palms and bathed the little camp in its pale glow. As Thorn walked into the clearing he saw the clan people bringing in armfuls of dead wood from the edges of the surrounding forest. They stacked it into many piles and set these ablaze, ringing the camp with fire.

Thorn knew they too had heard the roar. Once again the women and the elders would shun the deep woods and the far banks of the river.

Thorn made his way through the camp, past the little huts with their rancid odors of burning goose fat and fish oil. He heard the guttural voices of the clan people within, talking, arguing, coughing, the wail of a baby, a child laughing. He walked past the shaman's hut in the center of the clearing and on to the opposite side of the camp, where a long sandy path led far out into the grasslands.

He dropped his string of garfish to the ground and leaned against the stump of a broken cabbage palm, staring out across the moonlight savanna. Each time he came here he thought of the other Smilodon and the violent things that had happened. It was four summers past and he was not yet wandering the scrub and woodlands by himself.

Once again, he swallowed hard as memory stirred within him. In that special corner of his mind he could see the clan people gathering in little groups. He could still feel the giddy excitement as the small band of hunters made ready to leave. They milled about at the edge of the path leading out of camp. As was the custom, the women waited in small groups under the shadows of the fringe trees. Three of the younger women, of perhaps fifteen or sixteen summers, held babies in their arms. They waved and called in nervous voices to the seven hunters standing in the bright sunshine.

As Thorn waited beside his father, his chest swelled with pride, for his father was Bitar, the chief, the leader of the clan. He was a big, stocky man with a round face and a great head of bushy black hair. He stood with the other hunters, his arm around Thorn's shoulders.

Oom, their best hunter, a young man, strong and tall, stood there too.

Thorn smiled up at him. "I would go with you if they would let me," he said.

Oom grinned, showing a flash of white teeth. He ruffled the boy's hair with a big hand. "One day soon you will be old enough," he said. "But now you must stay and take care of Nema. When we come back I will tell you what happened, and I will bring back the fangs of the evil cat. Together we will make knives, one for you and one for me."

The hunters' bodies were marked with brightly colored pigments. Seven had outlines of red snakes twined around their arms and legs. One had a heavy strip of mastodon hide wrapped around his left arm, to be used as a shield. Oom's chest was painted with a crude figure of a crested eagle to ward off the evil spirits. He wore a narrow headband made from the skin of an ocelot. Bitar alone was without markings. He wore a loose deerskin loincloth and a necklace of jaguar teeth as befitted a chieftain and leader.

Most of the hunters carried three long spears. Tipped with a keen-edged flint, each was sharp and deadly. Oom carried a special one, its spearhead carved from amber-yellow flint and tied to the shaft with a thin band of orange and black snakeskin.

Thorn waited quietly as Bitar raised his hand for silence. The big man spoke in a deep, powerful voice that carried out across the clearing. "Clan people," he said, "three times now, in as many days, the evil cat has taken a life—first, a woman searching for snails along the banks of the river, and then yesterday two hunters, killed while tracking a brush pig in the oak wood."

The big leader shook his head and glanced around at the people. Then he went on: "We can wait no longer. Our clan is small, our hunters few. We go to rid our village of this evil scourge. Pray to the spirits for good hunting and our safe return."

When he had finished, Bitar reached out and took the hand of the leading elder and pressed it between his hands. Then he gave the word, *"Shanti"*—safe hunting.

It was repeated by the elders, who came forward one by one to touch Bitar on the shoulder for good luck. "Shanti," they said. In the background the women took it up. The word passed from group to group and became a chant. "Shanti, shanti," they shouted.

Then Dour, the little shaman, made his way into the small group. His body was painted with red ocher, his face marked with streaks of yellow clay. The hunters towered over him as he sprinkled them with palm ashes, and they each leaned down for him to place an amulet of rattlesnake fangs around their necks to protect them from demons. He danced around them, his bare feet kicking up a cloud of dust, and then closed his eyes and lifted his bony arms in prayer, calling on the spirits to favor the hunt.

The hunters raised their flint-tipped spears over their heads. The broad blades caught the glint of the sun. The clan people shouted in unison, "Shanti, shanti," as the nine hunters turned and walked bravely out across the savanna to find and kill the evil cat.

Thorn watched until they disappeared, tiny dots against the horizon. All day he waited, restless and impatient. He played with a cattail reed, throwing it like a spear at a nearby bumelia bush, pretending it was Smilodon.

He could think of nothing but the hunters, for early in the morning Oom had told him how they would track down the big cat as he lay in the tall grass, resting from his midnight meal.

"We will surround the beast and walk up slowly, with out spears ready," said Oom. "We will shout and curse and taunt him until he becomes angry. Soon the madness will burn inside of him and he will rush out blindly and attack the nearest hunter. Then the spears will fly, one after another. Ten or twelve will reach their mark, and Smilodon will be impaled like a garfish. For a while he will thrash about charging, dragging the spears with him. Then he will grow weak and fall on his side. The spears will snap and bend beneath him. He will breathe heavily, then lift his head for the last time and try to roar. But his voice will gurgle in his throat and blood will spurt from his nostrils and he will die."

Thorn could not forget Oom's story, and he felt his heart beat fast as he told it over and over again to himself. But he was not with the hunters, so he waited and threw his cattail reed at the bumelia bush.

The morning passed slowly and Thorn continued to keep watch. The sun climbed high in the heavens and began its slow descent in the west as he paced back and forth along the edge of the camp.

It was late in the afternoon when he saw the tiny

brown figures returning. Like a line of tired warriors, they hobbled slowly, coming closer and closer.

Panting with suspense, Thorn ran through the camp. "They are coming!" he shouted. "They are coming!"

The clan people streamed out into the clearing, the elders taking up the front ranks at the foot of the path. They stared into the distance, waiting anxiously, and talked and gestured to each other. Closer the little band of hunters came. The elders held up their hands to shield their eyes from the setting sun. The hunters were returning, but something was wrong. Some of them were limping. Others were bent over, walking slowly and carrying a heavy burden.

Thorn stood beside Nema. She chewed nervously on her ague twig as the solemn procession approached. The boy watched in horror: the two leading hunters carried a man between two willow poles lashed together. He was limp, his arms hanging down, and the poles bent under his weight. Thorn winced. The man's body was slashed open from neck to groin. His head fell to one side and his eyes were dull and glassy. For a long moment the boy stared, trying to understand what had happened. Then he moaned, and his mouth dropped open in disbelief. The man was his father, and he was dead.

The boy's lips moved but no words came; his fists clenched tight at his side. A terrible pang of anguish swept through him. His small body stiffened and he started forward.

Nema held him back. "Stay," she said, her voice choked and trembling. "There is nothing you can do."

Thorn felt the pressure of her hand as it squeezed his arm. At eight summers he knew he was too old to cry out. He bit his lip and blinked hard and felt the warm tears run down his cheeks.

Moments later Oom came limping into the clearing. His young face was contorted in pain as he hobbled along, supported by one of the other hunters. A long gash ran down the length of his right arm and continued down his thigh. Blood still oozed from the livid scar. He moaned and turned his head from side to side.

Thorn stood silent and dumbfounded. He could not believe these things had happened. It was not the way Oom had told it. It was not what the spirits had promised.

Three of the elders came forward and helped Oom to his hut, where they laid him gently on a soft bearskin robe.

The boy continued to watch, glumly, almost without seeing, as the rest of the sad procession came in. Then he was shaken out of his stupor. For down the long path leading from the open grasslands came the last four hunters. They carried Smilodon's body on a rack of poles: a great tawny corpse, heavy muscular shoulders, and huge paws dangling limply over the side of the rack. Thorn stared at the long fangs covered with blood. Then he saw the spears, nine of them, piercing crisscross through the body. He was sure that one of them belonged to his father and another one must be Oom's.

Dour came out of his hut holding a stone bowl of smoldering titi leaves in one hand, shaking his turtle-shell rattle in the other. Streaks of red and yellow still covered his scrawny body. Once again he danced about and chanted to the spirits. "Oh, heart of the great cat, we have drawn your fangs. Do not let the demons be angry. Let the spirits rejoice. The people can live in peace again, and Great Claw and the other beasts can live without fear."

The four hunters carried the carcass of the great cat into the center of the clearing and set it on the ground. Nema immediately fell to her knees and began to skin it, for all meat-eating beasts were butchered and skinned before the sun went down, in order to keep their spirits from escaping into the darkness.

Dour and some of the clan people gathered around to watch. Thorn stood by Nema's side.

Nema spit out her ague twig and leaned over the dead beast. Holding her flint knife in both hands, she raised it high above her head. She grunted a vengeful oath and fell forward, plunging the knife deep into the chest of the animal. A hissing sigh of air came from the stab wound, as though the beast were dying for a second time.

The clan people murmured and fell back. Dour raised his eyes skyward and held up his scrawny arms. "It is a sign," he said. "The spirit of the beast has escaped."

Nema went on with her work. With firm, deliberate strokes of her knife she slit the beast down the belly, just as it had done to her son. Then she proceeded to slice away the skin. As she worked, tears ran down her cheeks and fell on her bloodstained hands.

Thorn knelt beside her and put his small arm around her waist. He pressed against her and felt the muffled sobs shaking her body.

Nema cut out the spears. The one with the amber-yellow flint and the orange and black band had pierced the heart of the great beast. She pulled it out and gave it to Dour.

When the skin had been removed, other women came and cut up the meat. They spread it out on layers of palmetto fronds, and the clan people came and stooped to take what they needed.

The heart was given to the hunters. They cut it into strips and ate it raw to gain new strength and courage.

The boy watched in stunned silence.

That was four summers before, but Thorn would remember it the rest of his life. He turned his eyes away from the moonlit grasslands and picked up his string of fish. Now another Smilodon walks the land, he thought. I must find a way to kill him.

·FOUR

THE SHAMAN'S HUT STOOD IN the center of the camp, surrounded by the other dwellings. Larger and sturdier than the rest, it was built in a circle of palm logs with arched ridge poles covered by slabs of oak bark and corkwood.

A fish-oil lamp flickered within. Thorn walked up quietly but did not enter. Inside, Dour was chanting. Thorn sat down outside and carefully lifted the flap of heavy mammoth hide that covered the entrance. He peered in and saw Dour's thin body outlined in the dim light. The shaman was sitting cross-legged on a reed mat, a saucer-shaped stone filled with smoldering sweet bay leaves in front of him. A thin column of white smoke curled up and drifted out through a tiny opening in the roof.

The little man's chest and arms were covered with a dull yellow pigment; his face was painted red with large white circles around his eyes. The dried head of an ivory-billed woodpecker was pinned to his knot of gray hair. As he rocked back and forth he sang a whining tune and shook a rattle made from an empty box-turtle shell filled with pebbles. "O evil one, I hear your spirit roaring in the night. I listen for the sound of your padded feet. I feel the anger of your breath on my back. Do not take your revenge on the people. Find the one who cast you into darkness. Him alone. He is here, he is here." Dour swayed back and forth in rhythm with the simple dirge.

Thorn watched through the crack of the open flap and listened to the eerie chant. Then his body stiffened and a knot of anger twisted in his stomach. Oom! *Dour calls on Smilodon to come and kill Oom.*

Suddenly the chanting stopped. The tent was still. "Who is there?" Dour asked.

Quickly Thorn got to his feet, his heart beating like a drum, and stood in front of the hut. He removed two of the fish from his string and held them above the entrance. He waited until the shaman had finished his chant, then called out. "Wise leader, keeper of the spirits, I bring you gifts from the river."

There was a long pause. Then the shaman answered, "What gifts do you bring?"

"Good fish from the still waters," said the boy.

"How are the fish called?" asked the shaman in a shrill voice.

"Garfish," said Thorn, "the one with the long nose."

The shaman snorted. "Ugh, there is more meat on a stick."

Thorn reached down and picked up the bowfin. He

thought about the eel, but he would not tell the shaman about that. And he would not tell him he had
heard his chant. He held up the bowfin. "Also a fat
mudfish," he said, "longer than my arm."

Dour grunted. "Very well," he ordered. "Take off
your sandals and come out of the darkness, clan boy.
Come help me speak with the spirits."

Thorn poked his burning torch upright into the
sand outside the hut. He removed his sandals,
stooped over and pushed his way through the narrow opening.

Inside, the hut was warm. Heavy odors of fish oil,
dried meat and sour fruit hung in the air. On the
sandy floor, near the walls, were shells filled with
nuts, bulging skin sacks of roots and tubers, rolls of
animal pelts, and many flint tools. Strings of dried
fruit, snail shell beads hung from the ridge poles, all
gifts of tribute to the shaman so that he might call
on the spirits to grant someone's wish or simply
bring good luck.

Thorn held up his offering of fish for the shaman's
inspection.

The little man grunted again and waved his
hand—a sign for Thorn to place them on the ground.
He stared at the boy, his green eyes strangely wild.
"The demon has come," he said. "You have heard
the roar of Smilodon?"

"Yes," said Thorn, "I saw his mark by the river."

"Ah, you see," said Dour. "It is as I have said, the
evil cat has returned to find the one who took his
life."

Thorn hesitated. He kept his eyes on the ground. How could he question the shaman? Yet Oom was his friend. His only friend.

"I was but a child," said Thorn. "But the day of the killing I remember many spears. Which one took the life of Smilodon?"

The old man sniffed. "Which one do you think?"

"Perhaps my father's?"

"No," said Dour. "The spear that pierced Smilodon's heart belonged to Oom. Of that I am sure."

"Then is it not wrong, wise one, to put the curse on Oom, the brave hunter who saved the clan from the evil cat?" said Thorn.

Dour shook his head and held up his hands in a gesture of denial. "Oom is my friend, as he is yours, boy. I put no curse on the man. He killed Smilodon. Yet he kept the skull, and the skin still lies in Nema's hut. None of these things did they destroy. I warned them of the omen but they did not listen. Now the ghost of Smilodon is back to seek revenge."

The boy felt a sudden twinge of fear. If this is true, then Nema is right, she too is in danger. She too is— He paused in the middle of his thought. "We can still bury the skull and burn the skin," he said hopefully.

"You cannot," said Dour. "It is too late. Already the evil one prowls the night searching for its spirit."

"Then we must kill the beast," said Thorn, intensely, "the way it killed my father."

"Your words are easy," said Dour. "But the deed is not. It took nine brave hunters to kill Smilodon the first time. A thousand cannot kill him now."

Thorn was startled. He shook his head in disbelief. "Why?"

"Because the cat is the spirit of Smilodon. You cannot kill a ghost. Such a demon can die only by its own doing."

"What if this cat is not a ghost but only a new Smilodon searching for a place to hunt?" said Thorn.

"Clan boy, I have seen the signs in my sleep and I have spoken with the spirits. I tell you what I have already told Oom. I do not question the spirits, and I will say no more." The shaman stood up and dismissed the boy with a wave of his hand.

Thorn turned to leave, but before he reached the flap opening, the shaman called after him. "Tell me, clan boy, where do you get these thoughts, from Nema?"

The boy looked back and shook his head. "No," he said. "From the spirit girl. She said this Smilodon is no ghost but only another saber cat searching for new hunting grounds."

The old man grunted, his eyes narrowed. "You spoke with this girl?"

"Yes, tonight, down by the river."

"Then you are a young fool," said the shaman, shaking a bony finger in the boy's face. "She is one with the animals. That is why the clan people fear her."

"But she is as you and I," said Thorn. "Why should the people be afraid?"

"Because she comes from the land of the Lake

Dwellers," said Dour. "They were great hunters, but they denied the spirits and laughed at the demons. They believed only in the spear. You are too young to remember." Dour paced to the back of the hut, then came forward again. "Perhaps it is time to tell you. Yes. Many summers ago the Lake Dwellers raided our camp and the camps of other clans. Worse, they stole the children and took them away to raise as warriors and hunters. It was a time of much grief for the tiny clan. It was the thing never spoken. But we do not forget. You were saved because Nema hid you for three days in the oak wood."

Thorn did not remember, but he nodded slowly. "So . . . then that is why we have so few hunters, and why there are no other people of my age in the clan." His head reeled from the thought.

"Yes," said Dour, "and that is why she is not welcome here or in any of the other clans."

"Why, then, does she walk alone?" asked Thorn. "Why does she not hunt with her people?"

Dour leaned down and sprinkled more bay leaves into the bowl of the smoldering incense. When he looked up his eyes were cold and vengeful. "They were punished for their evil ways by the very spirits they denied. Four summers ago many stories were heard of a strange sickness that swept across their land. Their people died in their huts, their hunters fell dead in the middle of the forest. No children were born. Even much of the game disappeared, the bison, the deer and the llamas. Now the land is barren and taboo."

Just then a large night moth came through the opening into the light of the hut. It flew straight into the flame of the hanging fish-oil lamp. There was a sizzling sound as its wings caught fire. It fluttered in a dizzy spiral, then fell to the floor, burned to death.

"You see," said Dour, "that is a sign, the way the Lake Dwellers died. The spirit girl is the only one who lived. For what reason she was spared, we do not know." The old man shrugged. His dark eyes squinted at the boy from within the white circles of paint. "Is it perhaps that the spirits—sent her here to do evil?"

Thorn shook his head. "This very night she warned me of Smilodon and said to have the people ring the camp with fire. Why would she give such warning and then plan to do harm?"

The old shaman leaned down and picked up a large black feather from the reed mat where he had been sitting. He tapped the quill end against his fingertips. "I am sure the girl is a changeling."

"A what?" asked Thorn, puzzled.

"A demon that changes form, from animal to man. By day she walks like a girl. By night she prowls like a cat."

Thorn was stunned. "A changeling?"

The old man pursed his lips and stared off into the distance. "I warn you, clan boy, if you walk with this girl you will be in danger."

Thorn waited to hear no more. He walked out into the night, his mind filled with many unanswered questions. He could not believe the girl was evil. Her face, her eyes, her hands, were the same as his or Nema's. No different, he said to himself. He shrugged his shoulders and picked up his string of fish. Then he strode to the other side of the camp to see Oom.

· FIVE

AS THORN WAS ABOUT TO enter the flintmaker's hut, a girl dressed in a light llama-skin robe, her hair tied back with a string of fever-tree flowers, stooped out. Thorn knew it was Ute, Oom's clan sister. She kept Oom's hut, prepared his food and sewed his skins and sandals. She nodded to Thorn in the dim light, then tiptoed off into the darkness.

Oom sat behind the huge skull of Smilodon. It was mounted on a palm log and served as a table and workbench. Knives, skin scrapers, stone hammers and hand tools lay scattered about him on the hard sandy floor, while long flint-tipped spears leaned against the walls. The old yellow tusk of a small mammoth together with leg bones of bison and horses stood in an upturned shell of a giant armadillo at the back of the hut.

Oom's brawny arms glistened in the light from the fire burning in the center of the hut. His long dark hair hung below his shoulders and a band of ocelot skin circled his head. Almond-shaped eyes and high cheekbones accentuated his brown face. A deep, ugly scar ran from his shoulder down his right arm, and along his thigh.

He walked with a limp and could no longer hunt and fish. He refused to be a burden to his people, so he had turned to flintwork and become the tool- and weapon-maker for the clan.

Oom was bent over his task when Thorn entered. With a sharp piece of flint he whittled out a spear thrower from a deer antler. He glanced up quickly, and the boy caught the dark, foreboding look in his eyes. Usually the young craftsman greeted him with a smile and listened eagerly as Thorn told about the day's hunting and fishing; Oom would tease him and call him "spirit of the river." But now, grim-faced, Oom turned back to his work, his head down.

Thorn stood impatiently, eager to speak. He ran his hand across the top of the massive skull. It felt cold and smooth. His other hand wandered down to one of the long fangs jutting out of the upper jaw, and his fingertips traced the outline of its sharp cutting edge. It was longer and sharper than Oom's spearheads.

How many times, when he was only a child, had he run his fingers over these long white fangs? How many times had he played on the floor with pieces of antler and a leather sack full of puma and jaguar teeth while Oom recovered from his wounds and worked quietly over his flints? As Thorn got older he

often ran to this very spot, panting and out of
breath, to tell Oom about a band of horses he had
chased across the savanna or the hundreds of tall
white cranes he had seen dancing in the grasslands.
    He was thinking now of the day he had dug up a
nest of alligator eggs and was chased off by the
angry female and how Oom had laughed until the
tears came to his eyes when Thorn had told him.
"Boy, you are luck's friend," he had said. Always
they talked about hunting and fishing, things they
both loved to do, things Oom could do no more. Yet
sometimes, when Oom got tired of his flintmaking,
he would hobble out along the trails and lay vine
snares and nooses; the next day Thorn would bring
in the catch, usually a river hog or an opossum. On
rare occasions they would catch a deer in one of the
big snares. Then the camp would eat well, and
Thorn and Oom would laugh and talk together long
into the night.

But tonight was different; tonight Oom was grim-
faced and withdrawn.

Thorn cleared his throat. He spoke softly, as if he
were waking a sleeping man. "Smilodon is back."

Oom did not answer at first. Instead he looked out
through the open flap of the hut, staring into the
night as though he could see the great beast prowling in the darkness. Then he said, in a low voice,
"Yes, I have heard his roar. He has come to kill me."

Thorn was stunned. It was not like Oom to talk
this way. "No, Oom," he said. "The Smilodon that
walks the forest tonight is not the ghost of the one

you killed. He is a rogue. He hunts for food. He does not look for you."

The young flintmaker looked up quickly. "Where did you hear this talk?"

"The spirit girl." Oom would know the thing never spoken. All this time. But Thorn went on. "She said the new Smilodon is real."

Oom grunted. "I do not believe that sister of evil. I believe only what the spirits say."

"You have talked with Dour," said Thorn. "You have heard his omen?"

"I have," said Oom, "as surely as I have heard the roar of the cat. He is a demon ghost." Oom held up his hands. "There is nothing I can do."

The boy was alarmed, puzzled by this sudden change. He had never seen Oom like this before. "But there is, Oom. The Smilodon that walks out there is only flesh and blood."

Oom shook his head slowly. "More talk from the spirit girl." He placed his hand on the big skull. "Here is the curse that brings the beast back. I have killed his spirit, and he will not leave until I am dead. So long as I live, the clan will be in danger."

Thorn too spread his hands on top of the skull and leaned forward. "No, that is not true. Even Nema will say it is not so."

"Nema is an old woman," said Oom. "She has seen many summers and much sorrow. She does not wish to think about these things anymore."

"Why do you say that?"

"Because Nema skinned the evil cat," said Oom.

"Each night you sleep on the pelt that lies in her hut. Is she not then part of the omen, boy?"

Thorn felt a chill creeping up the back of his neck. This was the second time he had heard these words. "I will not believe that," he said.

"But you will believe the spirit girl?"

"I will believe what is true," said Thorn. "I will not believe things that are false."

Oom stood up and brushed the antler chips from the apron skin he was wearing. "It is no use. The ghost of Smilodon is back. Soon he will come. I can sit here and wait, or I can go out to meet him."

"With what?" said Thorn. "You can no longer throw a spear. You cannot even run."

Oom shrugged. "I will stand in the cat's path and let him come. In this way the omen will be fulfilled."

Oom has changed, the boy thought. Never before would he talk like this. The shaman has filled his mind with demons and evil spirits.

Just then a loud roar echoed through the night. The chilling sound shattered the darkness and thundered through the little camp.

Oom's jaw tightened. "Hear now, he speaks. He prowls around the camp, taunting me to come out and face him. If I do not, then he will come here to find me—the people, even Nema and Ute, will be in danger."

"Wait," said Thorn, "there is still time." He motioned toward the entrance. "Look, the fires burn brightly. The camp is safe, at least for tonight."

"Why should I wait? Tomorrow will be no different." The young man limped around the boy and barged out through the entrance of the hut. He went without a spear, without even a knife.

Thorn's mind raced ahead. He followed Oom out into the night.

Ute was there, pacing back and forth in the darkness, wringing her hands nervously. "Stop him," she begged. "Oh, stop him."

Thorn ran on. He planted himself in front of the tormented man. "Wait, Oom, listen to me. Together we will find a way to kill the evil cat."

Oom shook his head and pushed his way past the boy. He hobbled along, heading for the open grasslands at the edge of the camp. "We cannot kill a ghost."

Once again Thorn ran ahead and placed himself in Oom's path. "But a ghost can die of its own doing, Dour says."

Oom glared down at him, his eyes wild and staring. "So?"

"So we can set a trap," said Thorn. "The way we do for the jaguar. You can make a great spear, ten paces long, sharper than a mastodon tusk and as strong as an ironwood tree."

Oom listened, but his face showed no interest.

Thorn went on. "I will dig a deep pit out on the open grasslands. Then I will plant the great spear in the center and cover it with palmetto branches. A dead tapir will serve as bait." The boy's eyes danced with anticipation. "Smilodon will see the vultures gathering and will come to feed. If he falls into the pit and impales himself on the great spear, will that not be of his own doing?"

All around the little camp the fires blazed high, crackling in the night breeze. Oom frowned. He stood for a moment, thinking, and the boy was sure he saw a faint glimmer of hope in the young man's eyes. "Maybe," said Oom, "maybe it is so. I will speak with Dour—see if such a thing will satisfy the spirits."

"Then you will not go out into the grasslands to-night?" Thorn asked hopefully.

Oom turned slowly and started limping back to his hut. "I will wait—see what the shaman says, boy."

Thorn watched as Oom stooped back through the narrow opening of his hut and sat down at his work-bench. He picked up a flint scraper and the antler he had been working on. The boy breathed a deep sigh. Oom was still not the friend Thorn remembered, but he knew the flintmaker would keep his word.

Then, once more, out of the darkness came the deep-throated, thundering roar.

SIX ·

SMILODON LIFTED HIS HEAD, sniffing at a ring of fire. The man smell was strong. He had smelled it before and found it hateful. But now he was hungry and it might mean food. Silently he hunched down in the tall grass and crept closer. He saw two human figures carrying bundles of wood and a smaller one leaning against the stump of a cabbage palm. They were all outlined against the glow of light. For a moment he gathered his legs beneath him, ready to charge. The distance was short. With a few bounds he could be upon them. Yet the smell of fire held him back. It was the one thing he feared.

Deep in the recesses of his primitive brain he remembered the time he chased a family of brush pigs through a grass fire, and he remembered the stabbing hot embers beneath his feet. The pigs, with their hard, stonelike hooves, had scampered over the hot earth with little discomfort. But Smilodon's sensitive paws were badly burned. And so he had learned.

Slowly he lifted himself to his feet. Slinking low, he circled the little camp and sought another way in. But everywhere he turned, his amber eyes caught the glint of fire, the orange-yellow tongues of flame that lit up the night and barred his way.

He turned away, leaving the little camp behind. He limped badly and could not hunt. He traveled slowly north. Frightened armadillos scurried away in front of him, swamp deer ran off at his approach.

For eight summers Smilodon had dominated a wide area of dry savanna, interspersed with wet hammocks of cabbage palm and bald cypress, all bordered by flatwoods of pine and scrub. Here small herds of mastodons still roamed and giant ground sloths browsed. Even a stray herd of mammoths occasionally wandered into the area.

As undisputed ruler of this wide grassland, the great cat hunted with a mate. Working together, they cleverly cut out the mastodon calves from the cows and the giant ground sloth yearlings from their mothers. They killed frequently, and each time they brought down a calf or sloth they fed well for three or four days before leaving the carcass to vultures and dire wolves.

Then one morning Smilodon heard the roar of another sabertooth. The growling roar carried far, yet it was not as deep and heavy as his own. As he had many times before, he trotted toward the sound to meet the challenge.

At six summers this newcomer was fully matured, in his prime. He carried his head high, and thick shoulder muscles rippled under his tawny coat. Four years previously he had left his mother's side to roam as a bachelor, feeding on scraps from the kills of jaguars and dire wolves.

Now his season had come and he wanted a territory and a mate of his own. He was willing to fight and risk his life for it, just as Smilodon had done eight summers before.

Smilodon saw the other cat come plowing through the shoulder-high grass, holding his head just above it. They came face to face. Threats of angry growls rumbled in their throats. They stopped a few paces from each other, then circled slowly. The old cat eyed his opponent, taking his measure. He was not quite as large as Smilodon and he was young. That meant he was brash and untried. It also meant he was fast.

Smilodon threw back his head. He dropped his lower jaw, fully exposing his great saber fangs, and snarled a vicious warning. This gesture alone was usually enough to drive away a bold intruder.

But the new cat did not run off. He felt an urge for dominance and he was ready to fight. He opened his jaws and held up his head, his flat snout wrinkled back in anger as he displayed his own deadly set of fangs.

Both cats bluffed for a moment, snarling and hissing, testing each other's will to stand firm. Neither gave ground. Both refused to be intimidated.

Now that threats and display did not work, Smilodon knew he would have to fight. With a savage growl he raised himself to his full height and charged. As he reached the intruder, he reared up on his hind legs and slapped out viciously with his great paws, catching the young cat on the shoulders and the side of the head. Quickly his opponent struck back, and Smilodon felt a series of hammerlike blows to his own head and shoulders. For a moment the great cats paced around each other, snarling and spitting. Again they reared up and slashed out with their long saber fangs, trying to draw blood. They snarled and growled, grappling and cuffing savagely with open claws.

Then, suddenly, they broke away from each other and backed off a few steps, pacing, eyeing each other in frustrated rage. Once again Smilodon rushed in, shoving and crowding. This time the young cat gave ground, letting Smilodon press the attack but at the same time striking with lightning-fast blows of his own sharp claws as he fell back. Often the young cat's jabs went wild, glancing off the thick hide and heavily muscled shoulders of Smilodon. Yet many landed with resounding thuds, stunning the old cat, wearing him down. He lay in the trampled grass eyeing his opponent, panting heavily, his pink tongue hanging out.

Frustrated by the young cat's stubborn resistance, he gave up caution and rushed in with reckless fury. He cuffed, he slapped, he pushed, using his superior weight to overpower the younger animal. He caught the intruder off balance and sent him crashing to the ground, rolling over and over in the dry grass. But the young cat sprang to his feet and came charging back. Time after time he rushed in, tough, tenacious, never seeming to tire.

Back and forth they battled, grappling, snarling, tumbling through the grass, churning up clouds of chaff and dust.

Then Smilodon hung back for an instant, looking for an opening. He drove in once more: swinging his head from side to side, he tried to slash his opponent in the throat or shoulder with his deadly fangs. But the young cat was quick; he spun around and dodged the blows.

The old cat felt the tiredness in his bones. His chest heaved and he waited, his legs splayed out. Suddenly the intruder charged, and the old cat felt the hot, searing pain as his young opponent caught him on the side with his long fangs, opening ugly gashes on his shoulder and flank. Blood spurted from the wounds and stained the grass as he rolled and tumbled across the ground with the younger animal.

They parted in a flurry of blows, with Smilodon reeling from side to side, his head hanging. He shook his head and snorted a spray of blood; then stood quietly, catching his breath.

But with a savage growl the newcomer was on him again, slashing for his throat. Little by little the old cat was forced back, stumbling, trying to keep his feet under him. The intruder pressed the fight. In short, quick rushes he came in, blinding the old cat, stabbing him, crowding him, never giving him a chance to rest. Blood spattered the ground as Smilodon fought on, tiring steadily, battling now as he had never fought before.

All the while, Smilodon's mate looked on, half hidden in the shadows of a palmetto shrub. She had no interest in the outcome. Without qualms, without a thought, she would accept whichever cat came away the victor. It was her way of life. She knew no other.

Doggedly Smilodon fought on; he used every trick, every wile he had learned in his long years of killing. It was not enough. At thirteen summers he did not have the stamina, the energy to go on. If he wanted to escape with his life there was only one thing to do—he must run. The next time they broke away from each other, the old cat turned and limped off across the grasslands. He moved blindly, giving up his territory without looking back. For some yards, the intruder followed, then, satisfied his opponent was defeated, stopped and turned toward his new mate.

On and on Smilodon went, breathing heavily, tired and weak from loss of blood. With his head hanging low, he traveled most of the day until he came to a partially dried-up water hole. He eased himself into the slimy green ooze and felt the coolness of it soothe his burning wounds.

The next morning he started north again: hunger drove him on. He searched for his usual prey, slow-moving mastodon herds or bands of clumsy ground sloths. But he found none.

That afternoon out on the grasslands he tracked two mastodons, one with a calf, and saw Great Claw, the giant ground sloth, browsing around the sand wallow near a hammock of cabbage palms. Although Smilodon was still a superb predator, they were too large and powerful for him to take on alone. Llamas, deer and bison were smaller and plentiful, but they were much too swift of foot. So he was forced to range far in search of prey.

Many suns passed. He lost weight, and his ribs began to show through his heaving chest. Now each faltering step made his slash wounds throb with pain.

Late one afternoon, his tired eyes saw a great bird circling low over the open scrub. He crouched patiently as the huge bird came lower and lower. In his early days as a bachelor, when he had hunted alone, he had learned that a condor or vulture flying low might mean food. He crept up slowly, lifting his head every few paces to search the open brush land. At first he saw only a mob of dark figures bobbing and leaping on the horizon. Then, as he crept closer, he heard the yelping and snarling and knew it for what it was. A pack of dire wolves had pulled down an old llama and were feasting on the fresh carcass.

Winded and half starved, he was in no condition to fight. But his empty gut overruled his sanity; he rushed in, snarling at the pack of scavengers. Taken by surprise, the wolves ran off to a safe distance and waited as Smilodon gorged himself on the warm, fresh meat. When he could eat no more he dragged his bloated body to a nearby hammock of palmetto bushes.

Twilight came and darkness settled over the scrub. A soft breeze sighed through the palmetto fronds. That night Smilodon would sleep soundly, his tired bones rested and his gut full.

Then shortly after he fell asleep a small vampire bat alighted on the ground beside him. Black as night, with dark beady eyes, it glanced around like a tiny, frightened gnome. For a long moment it waited, studying the sleeping animal. It watched the slow breathing movements and detected the radiating warmth. Nervously the bat looked around again. When it was satisfied that all was safe it hopped into the air, its velvet wings flapping silently. Then it landed on the cat's side, as gently as a drifting feather.

Guided by the smell of blood, the bat stepped lightly across the body of the sleeping cat until it came to the jagged gash on the cat's flank. With tiny incisor teeth, sharp as new knives, it scratched a spot on the open wound. Saliva, containing an anticlotting agent, dripped from the bat's mouth and entered the wound. Now the blood flowed freely and the little animal lapped it up with its long tube-shaped tongue, feeding until its tiny body was distended. The touch was light, and Smilodon slept on, completely unaware of the stealthy deed.

The loss of blood was insignificant, but the bat's

saliva introduced a rabid viral infection into the cat's bloodstream. The virus, an invisible particle that was neither plant nor animal, would incubate in the cat's warm body. Then slowly, over a period of weeks, Smilodon would become mad, a menace to any living thing that crossed his path.

·SEVEN

SMILODON WAS GONE. For many suns his roar was not heard, and the life of the clan went on as before. But nightly, over his saucer of smoldering bay leaves, Dour called up the spirits and nightly the signs all said the evil cat would be back. The omen must be fulfilled.

Thorn was uncertain about the omen, but would the cat return? Probably. He made plans to set a trap, and for many days he hunted in the flatwoods and along the riverbanks for a young deer or a big river hog to serve as bait.

While there he dug for snapping-turtle eggs in the sandbars along the river. He caught pig frogs in the reed beds and from the palm apple trees he gathered handfuls of beautiful tree snails marked with bright spiral bands of red, yellow and black.

Thorn loved this land with its swamps and lakes, its wild grasslands and hammocks of cabbage palms.

In the quiet backwater pools of the river, big green dragonflies buzzed and swooped in wild circles, inches above the water, fighting for their hunting territories, flying into each other like angry hawks.

One day he went into the middle of the oakwood forest. The big curving branches of the trees were dappled with gray and yellow spots. He looked up, his eyes moving from tree to tree, studying the glints of light, when suddenly he saw a flash of speckled color, half hidden among the mass of hanging moss and varicolored leaves—a jaguar. If he stared at it, it was in plain sight. If he blinked his eyes, it disappeared for a moment. Yet it never moved: it lay there stretched out on a thick limb, its head resting on its paws, its yellow eyes staring down at him. Thorn had seen many before, but usually just a glimpse, a fleeting shadow—never like this.

He stood there looking up at the animal, smiling, not afraid. "Hello, cat," he said quietly. "You are like me. You hunt alone. But you have no stories to tell. Maybe it is better that way." For a long while he could not take his eyes away. Then, even as he watched, the cat disappeared, as if swallowed up in the moving spots of sunlight.

Another day Thorn picked a trumpet flower for Nema. Proudly he carried it home across the scrub, when all at once he heard a whir of wings and out of the sunlight came a tiny red and green hummingbird. It hung in the air a hand's length in front of his face, sparkling like a living emerald. Daintly it poked its long bill into the flower. Thorn stopped to let it feed. When it was finished it flew backward, hovering for a moment as if dangling on the end of a string. Then it darted off to find another flower.

These exciting things were all around him, and he saw new ones every day. He saw the tracks of pumas that prowled across the scrub, he saw black bears scrounging for hackberries in the swamp thickets. Once, during a dry spell, he even saw a big white-faced cave bear going down to the river to paw for catfish in the oozing mud holes.

Sometimes he was so filled with joy at the sight of these things he wanted to shout. He wished he had a friend to share it with, but now he had none. There was Ute, but she was always busy sewing skins, preparing food and taking care of Oom. So all Thorn could do was hold his beautiful thoughts inside of him until he got back to camp to tell Nema.

Days passed, and Thorn still had not found the needed bait. One morning he started out early. He stepped cautiously around the fat, lazy water moccasins sunning themselves on floating moss-covered logs. In the swamp full of towering cypresses, he heard the high-pitched *kank, kank* of ivory-billed woodpeckers as they swooped from tree to tree in their endless search for wood grubs. Along the river he saw small flocks of scarlet ibis probing for crawfish in the mudbanks, and in the tiny clearings he watched large emerald-green silk spiders weaving their half-round webs to trap fluttering damselflies and bumbling palmetto bugs.

A fat river hog was what he needed, he was convinced. He walked along the banks past the reed beds and around the clumps of pickerelweed, searching. Schools of topminnows scurried away from his shadow, and here and there a mud turtle plopped into the water at his approach.

He made his way around a bend in the stream and came to a quiet backwater pool surrounded by a thicket of overhanging dahoon trees. Then, suddenly, across the way, he saw a young tapir feeding in the middle of a raft of water lettuce. It was a yearling, not much bigger than a fawn.

This was a bit of luck he had not expected. If the animal did not frighten and run off, it would be an easy catch. He stood quietly, hardly daring to breathe. Slowly, very slowly, he laid his spear on the ground. Then silently, step by step, he moved closer. He leaned forward and braced himself, ready to pounce.

Unaware of the danger, the tapir continued to feed. Thorn poised slightly above it and waited until it reached down into the weeds. Then, with a wild leap, he flung himself at the little animal. Just as he jumped he heard a loud shout of alarm from across the river.

Instantly the tapir spun around. Thorn's hands reached out for it. His fingers closed on wet matted fur, covered with mud. The little tapir squealed and squirmed. Thorn held on tightly as he was pulled across the weed bed, but water and slime splashed against his face, and he groaned as he felt the little animal slip out of his grasp. One moment he had it, the next moment it was gone. The tapir dove into the water and disappeared, leaving the boy empty-handed, lying facedown in the weeds.

Save for the low buzzing of dragonflies and the gentle swirl of water, the pond was quiet. Thorn cursed under his breath. He pulled himself to his feet, wiping mud and weed from his face. He looked around, baffled.

Then he heard a high-pitched giggle from the clump of dahoon trees. A moment later Fonn stepped out of the shadows. She stood on the far bank, her head thrown back, laughing.

Thorn felt the heat of anger rise in his cheeks. He turned on her in fury, temper flashing in his eyes. "Demon," he burst out, "why did you do that? Are you mad?"

"Do not be angry," said Fonn.

"Angry," Thorn sputtered, "why should I not be angry? If you had not frightened the tapir off, I would have caught him."

The girl laughed again. "For what? You are the great hunter. Why do you pick on the little one?"

The girl's crow, perched overhead in the dahoon trees, called raucously, ca-ha, ca-ha.

Thorn was sure the bird was laughing at him. He waded across the pool, still wiping mud and weed from his face and shoulders. He realized he was angry not so much because he had lost the tapir but because this fool girl had caught him off guard again. "So that is why you chased the tapir away?"

"Yes," said Fonn. "I have watched the young one

for many days. Its mother was killed by a jaguar. It has little chance to grow up, so I help it when I can."

"I did not want to kill it," Thorn snapped. "I meant to keep it alive, as bait, to trap Smilodon."

"Smilodon is gone," said the girl. "He will not be back for some time."

The boy glared at her and tried to calm the anger in his voice. "How do you know that?"

Fonn lifted her nose and sniffed like a cat. "He has not marked his trail for many days," she said. "All his tracks are old now."

"Maybe so," said Thorn. "But our shaman says he will return."

The girl nodded. "The cat hunts in a big circle. But your shaman is right, one day he will be back."

"Then I will need bait," said Thorn.

"Garfish make good bait," said the girl. "Under the morning sun the smell carries far."

Thorn shrugged. This girl thinks she knows everything, he thought. Then he remembered she was the daughter of Mogon, the great hunter. He walked up the bank to where Fonn was standing. It was the first time he had seen her in daylight. Her eyes were dark and slanted, her cheekbones high. Soft otterskins covered her body. They looped over one shoulder and hung down to her knees, and were tied at her waist with the skin of an indigo snake. A gleaming white knife, fashioned from the long fang of a saber cat was tucked under her belt, and a leather sack hung from her waist. She carried no spear. She wore no amulets or bracelets. Thorn studied her face for

a moment. He guessed her to be about fifteen summers. "You have been following me again?" he said.

"No," said Fonn. She glanced up into the tree
where the crow was still calling. "My bird, Shadow,
tells me when you come."

The boy smiled grudgingly. "How long have you
walked with the crow?"

"Two summers now," she said. "I found him as a
fledgling, fallen from the nest. Sometimes he talks
too much." She chuckled as she reached up and
broke off a twig from the branch of an overhanging
dahoon tree. "But he is a good friend, and he warns
me of danger."

There was a long silence. Then Thorn spoke of the
thing that was on the tip of his tongue. "You hunt
alone because your clan died in the great sickness?"

The girl gazed off toward a group of cabbage
palms, as if the answer lay somewhere in the distance. "Yes, all died, Mogon, everyone. I am the only
one left."

"Why do you not join another clan?"

"I have walked alone for almost four summers
now. Wherever I go the people chase me away."

Thorn felt a twinge of pity for the girl. He too
walked by himself and knew how lonely it could be.
"Maybe it is because your hunters raided the other
clans," he said. He could feel Dour's bitterness as he
spoke. "Many times they carried away the children.
The people do not forget."

"It is true," said Fonn, shaking her head sadly and
holding up her hand as a zebra butterfly fluttered

past. "Mogon was not a bad man, but he lived by the spear. He thought that to believe in magic and the spirits was weak and foolish. So he took the children and taught them to be strong, to live free and without fear." She glanced at him. "I know, because I am one of them."

Thorn looked at her in surprise. "You mean . . . ?"

The girl nodded. "Mogon was not my father. I was taken from the Sea People and raised by the Lake Dwellers. Mogon taught me to hunt and take care of myself. That is why I can walk alone."

Thorn smiled, a glint of hope shining in his eyes. "If you are not the daughter of Mogon, maybe our clan will take you in. Another young person to help with the gathering and hunting would be good."

"No," said the girl, "twice I have been near your camp and the elders have driven me off with stones."

Thorn realized she was right. The elders would not change their minds. Dour would chant over his smoldering bay leaves and call her a bad omen. So for now it could not be.

The girl pulled a leaf from a titi bush and began shredding it thoughtfully in her fingers. "It is the same wherever I go," she said. "Because I did not die of the sickness and because I walk with Great Claw and the mastodons, they think I am evil."

"They call you the spirit girl."

Fonn's dark eyes flashed in the sunlight. "I am no spirit." She shrugged. "That is what they want to believe."

The boy was silent for a moment, deep in thought. Then he turned to her. "It is true, not everyone can walk with the animals. When I get close, they run away. Ground doves, turkeys—I must creep up on them to hit them with stones."

"Because you are a hunter. You wish to kill. So they run or fly away."

"Yet you were taught by Mogon, the greatest hunter of all."

Fonn nodded. "From the time I was five summers I followed Mogon. I began to understand why the animals were afraid. Watch them. You will see the mastodon does not fear the giant sloth. The giant sloth is not afraid of the longhorns or the tapir. The deer and the llama walk among them all without danger. Because they are not hunters they walk peacefully side by side."

She waved her hand toward the horizon, indicating the forests and grasslands. "But if Smilodon or the jaguar or the dire wolves come, the other animals flee or stand ready to defend themselves."

"So if I were not a hunter, I could do as you do?"

"Yes," said Fonn, "but it takes a long time."

"And this can also be done with Smilodon?"

Fonn shook her head vigorously. "No, never. Nor can it be done with the puma or the jaguar. Like Smilodon, they are born with the weapons to kill. They can never change."

Thorn was puzzled. It is strange, he thought, people can change and become friends of the animals because they are not born with a spear or a knife. He smiled quickly. "It is good that there are not more Smilodons."

"Yes," said Fonn, "but long ago there were many. There were also many more mastodons and giant sloths, and huge beasts with shells almost as big as the huts in your village."

Thorn's eyes stared in wonder. "How do you know this?"

"Because I have seen them."

The boy frowned and looked at her curiously.

Fonn laughed. She hopped up on the low branch of a hackberry tree and sat there swinging her legs. "You think I do not tell the truth," she said. "Someday, when you come with me to my country, I will show you the thunder beasts and saber cats that lived a hundred summers ago."

·EIGHT

THORN COMPLETELY FORGOT the old shaman's warning about the girl. Day after day he and Fonn roamed together across savanna and scrub.

One morning he met the girl again down by the river. It was cool, and a steamy mist hung over the water. They spent a few minutes weaving palm-leaf nets from palmetto fronds, and then waded into the shallows to catch minnows. They splashed through the water, chasing the little fish up and down the stream, laughing, making fun of each other's clumsiness.

Shadow flew overhead calling *ca-ha, ca-ha,* as if he were laughing with them.

The tiny minnows were elusive, sometimes hiding under the banks, sometimes dashing between Thorn's legs, always darting from one place to another. Thorn and Fonn rushed after them, trying to scoop them out with their hands or catch them in the nets. But the minnows dodged around their nets and disappeared like tiny ghosts.

Fonn sat on the bank for a moment as Thorn moved back and forth across the stream. Knee-deep in the swirling water, he waded along the bank, slipping and stumbling on the moss-covered stones. Each time his net came up empty. Once he caught a small mud turtle. With a disgusted groan he let it go.

"Clan boy, you are a great fisherman," said Fonn, laughing, "but where are the fish?"

Thorn shook his head and frowned. He stretched out his arms. "I tell you I have caught bowfin as big as this."

Fonn wrinkled her nose and held up her little finger. "But you cannot catch a minnow as small as this?"

For a moment Thorn bristled. He started to snap back, then caught himself and smiled. "Someday I will bring the fishing line that Oom made and I will catch a tarpon as big as you."

It was almost noon when they stopped to rest. Tired and out of breath, they sat on the bank talking.

Then Fonn saw glints of silver flashing in a small pool just below the bank. "Look," she said, "shiners, a whole school of them."

Thorn saw them too. "Wait," he said, pointing to the narrow opening of the little pool. "Hold your net here to keep them from getting out." He looked at her with a knowing smile. "Now I will show you how to fish."

Fonn waited near the edge of the pool. She held the net in place to block off the entrance while Thorn climbed up into a nearby stand of woods. He searched hurriedly until he came to a group of small trees with dark palmate leaves. Greenish-brown fruit pods the size of crab apples hung from the branches. Thorn gathered as many as he could, pulling them off the low-hanging branches and placing them in his palmetto net.

When he had all he could carry, he ran back to the river, dropping some on the way. At the river he pried the pods open with his flint knife and dug out the chestnutlike seeds. These he placed on a flat rock and proceeded to smash with a heavy stone, producing a thick white pulp. Quickly he scooped up the pasty mixture and waded out to where Fonn was waiting. Then he leaned over the pool and sprinkled the shredded mash into the crystal-clear water. The little fish darted back and forth in panic as the bits and pieces sank to the bottom of the pool.

"Oom taught me how to do this," Thorn whispered.

Fonn watched. She saw the water begin to turn a thick, creamy white. Soon the fish and the entire contents of the pool were hidden beneath a cloud of milky water. She shook her head in wonder. "Where are the fish?" she said. "How will we catch them if we cannot see them?"

"Wait," said Thorn, "now you will see."

A few moments later the shiners began to float to the surface, belly up. Thorn scooped them out with his hand and placed them in his net.

"You have poisoned them," said Fonn.

"It is not a bad poison," said the boy. "We will take what we need. Then we will open the pool and let the others go. When they reach the clear water they will soon wake up."

Fonn helped, scooping up the little fish as quickly as they came to the surface. Soon their nets were filled, with twenty or thirty of the little fish, all flat and silvery, each one like a shiny hickory leaf.

When Thorn and Fonn were finished they opened the entrance of the pool and let the water run out. They carried their catch up to dry land and sat down to rest.

"Now we have fish to eat," said Thorn.

Fonn grinned. Her brown arms shone in the sunlight. "We need ground beans."

Thorn looked around, puzzled. "It will take a long time to gather enough."

The girl wrinkled her nose. Her dark eyes danced with humor. "Not if you know how," she said. "Come, it is my turn to show you a secret."

They folded the fish in the palm nets and started off along the riverbank. Thorn felt a new surge of joy. It was good to be running with a friend instead of hunting alone.

After a while they turned up through the flatwoods, where scrub jays scolded them from the tops of tall pines. Their nimble feet kicked up sand as they jumped over prickly cactus and dodged around palmetto shrubs. A pine lizard scurried across their path, and twice flocks of sand grouse flew up at their approach. On and on they ran, laughing and shouting to each other as they raced beneath the dappled sunlight of the open pines.

Shadow followed, flying overhead, shouting, talking too much.

Soon they came to a small pond near the edge of open grassland. Fonn stopped and held up her hand. "Here we will find our ground beans," she said.

Thorn looked about, still puzzled. He saw the clumps of palmetto shrubs and the scattered pine trees giving way to the grasslands, which stretched off as far as he could see. Where are the ground beans, he wondered. He glanced at Fonn, the question in his eyes.

The girl smiled. Tossing her long hair back over her shoulder, she stepped a little way into the meadow. She walked through the knee-high grass leaning over, searching from side to side. Soon she found a small round ball of dried grass, about the size of an apple, neatly woven in amongst the stalks of field grass.

"The nest of a meadow mouse," said Thorn.

Fonn gently poked her finger into the soft ball of grass. At once a little mouse hopped out on the opposite side. It squeaked faintly, then jumped to the ground and scurried off, disappearing among the roots and tangled vegetation.

Thorn watched as the girl tore a small hole in the nest. She held it open for him to see. It was filled with many small, round ground beans, each the size of a pea. She scooped out a handful and spilled them into her leather sack. Then she carefully closed up the little nest and stood up.

The boy frowned. "But there are still more inside," he said.

"Yes," said Fonn, "but we must leave some for the mouse. It is to show our good heart."

Thorn smiled. None of the clan people he knew ever spoke this way, not Oom, not even Nema. He reached out and touched the little nest with the tips of his fingers. It felt warm and soft. He looked up at Fonn. The shaman is wrong, he thought; this girl thinks of the animals as brothers and sisters. She is one with them. But she is not evil, she is no changeling.

They waded farther into the grasses, finding nest after nest all along the edge of the grassland. Soon Fonn's leather sack was overflowing with the small brownish beans. "Come," she said, her dark eyes beaming with satisfaction, "now we have enough." She led Thorn to a large clump of palmetto shrubs a short distance away. She pushed aside the fronds and uncovered a cache of flints, a gourd of tinder and a small skin sack for cooking.

Thorn was surprised. "You knew these were here."

"Another secret," said Fonn, laughing. "I keep many things hidden away in the scrub and oak wood so they will be there when I need them. If the armadillos and raccoons don't find them first."

They gathered scraps of palm wood and placed them in a pile. Then Fonn knelt down and removed a small bit of tinder from the gourd. She picked up her fire stones and struck them together. Sparks flew down into the tinder. Again and again she struck the stones together. Soon a few of the sparks settled on the dry fibers. Now Fonn picked up the tinder in her hands and began to blow on it. A thin coil of white smoke rose from within. She blew again and again. Suddenly the tinder burst into flame. She tucked it quickly under the pile of palm wood and continued to blow. A small flame licked up. It caught on the dry wood and the fire was started.

Next Fonn filled the cooking sack with water from the pond. She added the beans and hung the sack over the fire from a tripod of green willow sticks, then she placed a large flat stone close to the fire and laid the small fish in a long row on top of it. It wasn't long before the beans were boiling in the sack and the fish sizzling on the fry stone. Thorn collected tender stalks of bracken and Fonn stirred them in with the beans for seasoning.

While they waited, they went back into the scrub. Here they found a small date plum tree and picked some of the sweet yellow fruit to go along with their meal. Fonn plopped one into her mouth, chewing it thoughtfully. "Good," she said, "juicy and sweet."

When the feast was ready, they sat cross-legged on the sandy ground and took turns scooping out handfuls of beans from the warm cooking sack. With small pointed twigs they speared the little fish from the fry stone. The fish were crisp, brown, and tasty.

"Mmm." Thorn licked his fingers with loud smacking sounds.

During the meal Thorn told Fonn about Nema. "She is like a mother," he said. "She sews my skins and my sandals, and cooks the game and fish I catch.

Sometimes we fight and she scolds me. But when I am away for long I miss her, and it is good to go back and see her again."

Fonn gazed off into the distance. "You are lucky to have such a one," she said. "I was taken from my mother and raised by the women of Mogon."

"Even now the clan people talk of the Lake Dwellers with fear," Thorn said. "They call it an evil place. Because of the sickness, our shaman says it is taboo."

"The sickness is no more," said the girl. "It was over more than three summers ago. Now it is safe. I go there often. You see I am not sick."

"I believe this," said Thorn. "Yet the shaman calls you an evil spirit, a changeling."

The girl laughed. "All shamans are mad. They see things that are not there. They hear voices that do not speak. In our clan we did not have a shaman. Mogon would not permit it. He said they are all timid men. They know only how to chant and frighten the people." She looked at the boy, a faint smile on her lips. "But it is good you tell me of this. Now we can walk together as friends and I will trust you."

A friend, Thorn thought. A good friend.

After the meal Fonn hid her cooking utensils beneath the palmetto shrub and they started back for the river.

They had not gone far when Thorn noticed a gathering of vultures soaring low over the grassland. Something is dead, he thought, or is about to die.

The girl followed Thorn's gaze and frowned. "Listen!" she said.

Thorn heard it too, a long, drawn-out moaning sound, like the bawling of a lost bison calf. It seemed to come from far out on the grasslands, from an isolated hammock of gumbo trees and cabbage palms.

Fonn turned her head to one side, listening intently. Then her eyes lit up in recognition. "It is Great Claw," she said. "He is in trouble."

NINE ·

GREAT CLAW, THE GIANT ground sloth, stood hip-deep in oozing sand, his back legs and heavy tail mired in the marshy wallow. He was an awkward, oversize giant. Dim-witted and clumsy, he had allowed himself to be cornered by a roving pack of dire wolves.

Although he towered over them, the wolves knew he was trapped and they sensed an easy kill. They sprang and leaped, snapping at his haunches, his flanks and his long hairy arms, forcing him deeper into the quagmire.

Great Claw fought back viciously, lashing out with his sickle-like claws. Already two of the big wolves lay dead and bleeding at his feet.

Great Claw resembled a huge bear with small ears; he had tiny sad-looking eyes and the long face of a horse. With his heavy hind limbs and thick, stocky tail he could rear up to feed or defend himself. A frontal attack was unlikely, for Great Claw was protected by a tough mat of hard nodules embedded in his chest. Not even Smilodon's saber fangs could penetrate that thick layer of bony armor.

But now, ponderous and clumsy, he stood there slowly sinking in the sandy ooze, fighting for his life.

With powerful, bone-crushing jaws the big wolves moved in. Usually they sought less dangerous prey, young llamas or stranded river hogs. Often they preferred to search the skies for signs of vultures that might lead them to a crippled bison or a dead mammoth.

And so they had found Great Claw mired in this bog. Now, like a swarm of pesky flies, they leaped and snapped around him, forcing him deeper into the wallow. Great Claw thrashed and floundered as he sank deeper and deeper. He bawled out his strange plaintive cries and lashed back at his tormentors.

Thorn and Fonn heard his call and hurried toward the wallow, near a hammock of palm and fig trees. They plunged through the waist-high grass, scaring up clouds of grasshoppers and reed birds. The girl ran ahead and Thorn raced close behind her. They dodged around the low palmetto bushes and leaped over fallen palm logs.

Like the trumpeter of a coming storm, Shadow led the way. He swooped overhead and bustled with excitement, shouting his boisterous challenge—*ca-ha, ca-ha, ca-ha.*

Small bands of llamas ran off at their approach. A pair of red-capped cranes flapped hurriedly into the air, followed by a great flock of squawking grackles that had been feeding on the ground.

Thorn raced on, his feet crashing through the grass as he tried to keep up.

The moaning cries grew louder and soon Thorn could see the giant beast, bogged down in the wallow, desperately trying to fight off the growling pack of tormentors. His shaggy fur was ruffled up in anger. With wild swings he slashed out at the chomping wolves. He caught one in midair and flung it to the ground. Another slash of his big claw disemboweled it and in an instant it lay with the other two, dead at his feet.

The seven remaining wolves continued the attack. Much lighter than the sloth, they could dash along the edges of the wallow without sinking in. They snapped and harried Great Claw, and their wily instincts told them the old giant was tiring fast.

Great Claw swiped at them wildly. He could easily fight them off from the front, but he could not protect himself from behind.

Thorn and Fonn neared the spot just as the wolves tore and pulled at the animal's shaggy haunches. The pair stopped a short distance away to catch their breaths.

The wolves turned quickly. They snarled and bared their teeth. They came toward Thorn and the girl, slinking on their bellies, growling.

"Be careful," said Fonn, "the wolves have a meal. They will not be scared off so easily." Her eyes narrowed in anger. "They are like sparrows mobbing an eagle. If Great Claw were free they would not dare attack him."

The big wolves came on brazenly, heavy powerful brutes, lips curled back in anger, glaring at the boy and girl through yellow slitted eyes. The animals crept forward, growling viciously. Even as they crouched low, ready to charge, their heads were as high as the boy's waist.

Thorn had his spear and his knife. Fonn had only her knife. If the wolves came on together, Thorn knew that he and Fonn would have little chance to defend themselves. Without waiting, he moved a step closer and raised his spear, hoping the wolves would run. But they only crept closer.

Thorn felt a knot of fear in the pit of his stomach. He forced himself to remain calm as the snarling beasts moved within range; then with careful aim he hurled his spear at the nearest wolf. The animal leaped aside but the weapon struck a grazing blow on its flank. It yelped and limped off into the high grass, leaving a trail of blood.

The remaining six animals came on, snarling, yapping, bearing down on Thorn and Fonn.

Fonn shouted and waved her arms over her head, hoping to scare them off. But the wolves refused to be intimidated. After a moment's hesitation they came on again, grumbling in their throats. Like huge, sulking dogs they inched forward, slinking on their bellies, closer and closer. Two of them led the way, frothing at the mouth, chomping and snarling.

Thorn backed up slowly. His spear was far out of

reach now. He looked around in desperation for a stone, but all he saw were the tufts of yellow grass. Then he noticed a stick of palm wood a few steps in front of him. He picked it up, hefted it in his hand and stepped closer, then threw it just as the lead animal was about to spring. The stick tumbled through the air and struck the beast on the shoulder. The big wolf yapped and stumbled backward. It stopped for a moment, spread out its front legs and bristled with anger. Then, undaunted, it came on again, followed by the others.

Thorn reached for his flint knife. He held it nervously in the damp palm of his hand. He could use it to stab and slash and cut, but if all the wolves came on at once it would do little good. He knew he would have to throw it. If he missed he would have nothing left to fight with but his bare hands. He had to make up his mind quickly.

The wolves sensed the moment of indecision. They spread out, two of them circling behind until the boy and girl were surrounded.

Thorn felt beads of sweat forming on his brow. Now they were threatened on all sides. He saw Fonn move closer to him. She had her knife out too. She spoke under her breath. "Ready," she whispered.

Thorn raised his arm, holding the flint knife in full view. The lead wolf caught the movement and hesitated. Little by little the boy moved his arm back. Fonn did the same.

The lead wolf stopped. It lowered its head, its yellow eyes menacing. For a long moment it looked directly at Thorn, staring him down. The other wolves began to close in, a step at a time. The boy held his breath, waiting. He felt his heart pounding in his chest. He glanced at Fonn. She gritted her teeth, her eyes wide and staring. She stepped forward and whispered in a shaky voice, "Ready."

Thorn lifted his arms high. The ring of wolves moved closer, almost to their feet now. He saw the lead wolf brace itself, about to spring.

"Rush at them!" Fonn said.

Together the boy and girl leaped forward, shouting, flinging their arms wildly. At the same time Thorn threw his knife. It flew end over end and struck the lead wolf squarely in the face. The animal howled and ran, and rubbed its bloody snout in the grass. Fonn's knife hit another wolf in the chest. It stumbled, then slowly backed away.

The other wolves hesitated, uncertain, as their wounded companions loped off across the savanna. The rest of the pack milled around for a moment, snarling and growling. Then they too turned and ran. Their dark gray shadows vanished into the tall grass, leaving the savanna strangely quiet.

Thorn walked over and picked up his spear and his knife. He noticed his hands trembling and he turned and looked at Fonn. She gave a deep sigh and shrugged. Then together they threw back their heads and laughed, and Thorn felt a surge of wild elation.

With the wolves gone, Fonn went up to Great Claw. She walked beneath him, unafraid, like a cub pattering between the paws of a mother bear. The

giant sloth looked down at her, and talked in his
bleating, moaning voice.

She turned to the boy, a worried frown on her
face. "He cannot get out. He will only sink deeper."

Thorn looked around. The hammock of palms and
gumbo trees was only a few steps away. "We can
gather brush and throw it in front of him."

"And bundles of grass," said Fonn. "We must be
quick."

Together they went into the hammock, where they
picked up armfuls of dead branches and palmetto
fronds. They pulled up dried grass and rolled it into
bundles, then threw everything into the wallow in
front of the mired animal. They made trip after trip,
until the mass of dried vegetation was piled into a
thick, matted blanket.

Great Claw seemed to know what they were doing.
He moaned softly as he waited, his shaggy brown
shoulders leaning over them, his sad tiny eyes
watching whatever they did.

Next they tore limbs from the gumbo trees and
threw them on top of the mound of grass and brush.
When the pile seemed high enough they stepped
back and waited.

The giant sloth leaned forward. He reached over
with his big claws and hooked them into the tangle
of branches. Then slowly, very slowly, he began to
pull himself atop the mass of vegetation. He struggled mightily and little by little began to climb up.
He was almost out when the pile started to sink under his great weight. He tried again and again, but

each time he floundered and with a moaning cry sank back into the oozing sand.

Fonn groaned. Thorn cursed under his breath. He glanced around again, trying to think of something else, something more solid they could add to the pile of brush to make it stronger. He went into the hammock and searched under the trees, and picked up a few more branches.

Suddenly, he almost tripped over a fallen palm log. It was bulky and heavy. He called Fonn, and together they carried it out to the wallow and threw it on top of the pile. They went back into the hammock and found another log. It was too heavy to carry, so they rolled it over and over until they reached the wallow, then tugged and pushed it up onto the floating pile of vegetation.

Once again the giant sloth leaned forward. He hooked his big front claws into the log and pulled.

Thorn held his breath, his fists tight at his sides. He glanced at Fonn and saw the strain on her face.

Slowly Great Claw's huge bulk rose out of the shifting sand. Thorn heard the gurgling slosh of water as the liquid sand reluctantly gave up its victim. With tremendous effort the sloth heaved himself up onto the mound of brush and logs. He weaved back and forth for a moment, balancing himself on his wet haunches. Then he stepped out onto dry land.

He stood there, looking around, blinking his tiny eyes, a great brown hairy beast rising up out of the earth. He looked down at the boy and girl and moaned softly in his peculiar way. Then he turned and shuffled over to the nearest fig tree. He pulled down one of the branches, and his long wet tongue coiled out and stripped off the leaves. He groaned with pleasure and began eating as though nothing had happened.

"Now you too are a friend of Great Claw's," Fonn said to Thorn.

With the giant sloth safe, the two made their way back to the river. They walked in silence for a while. Then Fonn turned. "I will leave you here," she said. "But I have been thinking, maybe someday soon we can go to the country of the Lake Dwellers."

Thorn felt his heart leap. It was the thing he had been waiting for.

Flocks of chattering parakeets were flying low, heading for their roosting areas in the dahoon trees, when Thorn got back to camp. He found Nema squatting on the floor of the hut, scraping the skin of an opossum he had brought back a few days before. He did not tell her about the wolves and the giant sloth, but he did say, "I walked with the spirit girl again today."

Nema chewed busily on her sassafras twig and continued scraping the skin. "I am happy you have someone to walk with."

"And to hunt with," said Thorn.

"But I do not know about this girl," said Nema. "Is it good or bad?"

Thorn sat on the soft tan pelt that covered the floor of the hut. "You do not think she is evil?"

Nema wagged her head. "From what you tell me, I see no harm in the girl."

Thorn smiled. "Then soon I will go with her to the land of the Lake Dwellers."

The old woman looked at him sideways. "It is taboo."

"The sickness is gone," the boy said.

"But it is far."

"Only two days."

"And two days back," said Nema.

Thorn stood. He looked into her upturned face and saw the fear in her eyes. He knew she would worry. Yet he knew he would go.

TEN ·

SMILODON STALKED FAR to the north of the clan country, hunting for prey that was dwindling in numbers and slowly disappearing. He searched through scrub and swamp but found no ground sloths and only two small herds of mastodons, both without calves. He saw a puma feeding on the carcass of a swamp deer. With an angry growl he chased it off and fed on the scanty remains. He ate whatever he could catch—frogs, catfish, opossums. Once he pounced on an unwary alligator. It was not large but it fought back, snapping and thrashing. He stabbed it a dozen times before the fight was gone from it, then dragged it into the shallows and began feeding even as the tail twitched with life. But it was cold, and not the blood meat he was used to. He ate what he could and left the rest for the garfish.

Even as he lay in the mud, the rabies virus in his bloodstream seethed and multiplied, tripling a thousand-fold. It found the tangled nerve endings in his muscles and followed them to the rich, nourishing fluids of his spinal cord. Now slowly, inevitably, it would reach his brain.

ELEVEN ·

FOR TWO DAYS THEY HAD traveled through hot, dry scrublands and tall pine forests. Now they stood on the threshold of a new land, a land Thorn knew only as evil and cursed, a land he had never seen before.

Because of the fierceness of the Lake Dwellers, because of all the stories about the strange sickness, the people of his clan had never come here.

Now Thorn looked out over a valley that stretched away as far as he could see. It was not a deep valley but it was wide, with sweeping views of tall magnolia trees and limestone outcroppings on either side.

He stood there for a moment as a light breeze brushed against his cheeks. He felt the cool air touch the dampness around his neck and shoulders.

Fonn stood beside him, smiling proudly. "Here begins my clan ground," she said, "the country of the Lake Dwellers."

Thorn knew how she felt; the land was beautiful—the twisted trunks of the great oaks, the long silver curtains of moss hanging from every branch, the scarlet bracts of the flame flowers. Flocks of redstarts and summer tanagers flitted through the trees, filling the high canopy with flashes of red, ringing the forest with their music. Orange and purple tree orchids grew in the crannies of fat curving branches.

He looked over the valley and breathed in deeply. The air smelled good, warm and sweet. This land is new again, he thought. When he glanced at Fonn and saw her brown face bright and smiling, he knew she was glad to be home.

Fonn waved her hand across the horizon. "How can anyone think this place is cursed?" she asked. "The birds sing all day, and there is much game, and lakes filled with fish."

Small herds of deer ran across the trail, the does hurriedly rounding up the spotted fawns, their white tails flashing as they hurried off like nimble dancers. Groups of wood bison browsed side by side with brush turkeys under the shade of towering hickory trees. But all of these animals Thorn had seen many times before. He reached out and nudged Fonn on the shoulder and laughed. "And also animals from a long time ago?"

The girl smiled. She wrinkled her nose. Then she threw back her head and laughed with him. "You think I speak like a shaman. But wait, you will see."

Thorn followed her down through the center of the valley. On either side pines and scattered clumps of red cedar grew between the outcroppings of limestone.

Shadow flew down from the trees and landed on Fonn's shoulder, cawing in her ear. He too was glad to be home.

They walked together, the boy and the girl, enjoying the coiled vines with their strings of yellow flowers, the pink and red calyx lobes of the fever trees. Thorn stepped over twining coral vines trailing across a floor of dried holly leaves. The bright colors were everywhere, underfoot and overhead.

They came to a little glade at the bottom of the valley, surrounded by holly and low stands of mountain laurel. Fonn glanced around. "We do not have far to go," she said, "but we have been walking all morning. This will be a good place to stop."

Thorn was grateful for the chance to rest. He sat down and stretched out his legs, cramped from the long walk. Then he unrolled the deerskin he was carrying. Inside were papaw fruit, nuts and dried fish, all wrapped in palm leaves. The girl took the skin sack containing her fire stones and tinder from around her shoulder while Thorn gathered a few sticks of dead oak wood. They did not have to speak to each other; they knew what to do. Soon they had a small fire going.

Fonn roasted the nuts in the hot embers. The fish were warmed on a flat stone.

The odor of the frying fish filled the little glade, whetting Thorn's appetite.

"Be patient," said Fonn, "I am hungry too."

Thorn grinned. "She reads my thoughts," he mumbled. "Maybe she is a spirit girl."

When the food was ready they sat on a ledge of

limestone and used sharpened twigs to pick up the warm strips of fish.

Shadow waited for his share. Fonn offered him a piece of fish. He snapped it up greedily, then flew back up into the trees.

Thorn and Fonn ate without speaking. When they were almost finished, Fonn said, "You spoke of your friend Oom many times, but I still know little about him."

The boy thought for a moment, wondering where to begin. Then he told her how his father and Oom had hunted together for many summers and how Oom was injured in the fight with Smilodon. "He is a good friend. But now I am afraid he will do a foolish thing."

Fonn tilted her head to one side, as if asking why.

"It is because he believes that Smilodon has returned to kill him," said Thorn. "He thinks he must fight the evil cat once again to save the clan."

The odor of the fish drifted up in the warm air. Thorn reached over with his sharpened twig and picked up another piece. He ate it slowly. He started to speak again, but hesitated.

The girl nodded and spoke for him. "The shaman thinks I am to blame?"

"Yes. Dour says you are Smilodon's ghost, come back to seek revenge on the one who took your spirit."

"Does Oom believe this also?"

"Only because Dour has filled his mind with demons and spirits. Now he thinks of nothing else."

"I am sorry," said Fonn, "but I am glad you do not believe in this foolishness."

"I know you are not a spirit," said Thorn. "But I do not know about Smilodon. When he comes back I will dig a trap and set it with good bait. Then let him come and die of his own doing. In that way the omen will be fulfilled."

Fonn smiled, knowingly. "There is no ghost and there is no omen," she said. "But the trap is a good thing. You and Oom will not be in danger, and the cat will be killed."

They lingered for a while over the rest of their meal, chewing on chunks of dried papaw fruit. They had stretched out on a rock, when they heard a movement in the bushes, followed by a deep-throated growl. Thorn jumped to his feet and reached for his spear. A moment later a huge bear charged out of the laurel bushes. It snarled and stood up on its hind legs, towering above them, sniffing and shaking its great furry head.

"Stand still," said Fonn, sharply. "Do not run, and do not throw the spear."

Thorn's eyes widened. His voice was filled with awe. "A cave bear. I have not seen one in a long time."

"It is White Face," said Fonn. "He is old and he does not see well. But he smells the fish."

Fonn glanced up and whistled softly. Shadow came down from the trees. He flew around the bear's head, cawing loudly. The shaggy beast swiped at him with its paw. Then it dropped down on all fours and began sniffing again, walking toward the smoldering fire.

"Move back slowly," said Fonn, softly.

Thorn did as he was told, backing up one step at a time. The girl moved with him.

As soon as they were far enough away, the bear shuffled up to the fire. It scraped the remaining fish from the warm hearthstone with its paw and ate them. It sniffed around the fire and found the roasting nuts. Gingerly it pawed them out of the hot ashes and ate them one at a time, crushing them in its strong jaws. When it was finished, it pushed its nose into Fonn's sack of fire stones and tinder and scattered them across the ground. Then it pawed at Thorn's empty deerskin. It found nothing else to its liking. Again it stood up on its hind legs like a great, shaggy old man.

Fonn took a step forward and clapped her hands. "Go," she said in a loud voice.

The bear stared down at her for a moment as if uncertain. Then with a snorting grunt it dropped down and ambled off through the dogwood trees.

"Poor White Face," said Fonn. "He is old and almost blind. Before many seasons have passed I think he will die."

Thorn shook his head in wonder. He had never heard anyone speak to a bear like this and chase it away.

"He is a friend," said Fonn. "I give him food whenever I can—deer meat, fish and fruit."

"He walks alone," said Thorn, "like Great Claw."

"Yes," the girl said, "there are not many cave
bears left. Already the small black bears are taking
over their hunting grounds."

Fonn leaned down and put out the fire, smothering
the embers with dirt. She picked up her sack of fire
stones and tinder and slung it over her shoulder.

They went on again, through tall stands of tupelo
trees. Here and there they passed small pools of
clear water that seemed to well up out of the earth.
They soon came to a series of white limestone ledges
half hidden behind a row of tall magnolia trees.
Thorn heard the soft splash of falling water. It came
from the other side of the trees. He followed the girl
as she pushed her way between rows of low palmetto
shrubs.

All at once they came upon a trickling waterfall.
It dropped straight down from an open grotto in the
side of the cliff and splashed into a deep pool of clear
blue water. The edges of the pool sloped downward
and were covered with a slick, green moss.

"Be careful," warned Fonn, "it is slippery. If you
fall in, it is almost impossible to get out."

Thorn peered down into the pool. His mouth
dropped open in shocked surprise.

Schools of reef fish, of many colors, were swimming about in the clear water. Blue and yellow
parrot-fish poked along the edges and nibbled at the
mossy rocks. Spotted eagle rays swam back and
forth across the pool, flapping their triangular fins
like giant underwater birds. Fat goggle-eyed groupers hung suspended in the depths, opening and

closing their mouths as they breathed, while a company of sleek brown sharks circled lazily around them.

Thorn was amazed. "I have never seen such fish."

"They come in with the salt water that flows under the ground from the sea not far away," said Fonn.

The boy stepped back, still wide-eyed. He looked up at the grotto from where the dripping waterfall came. It was almost as high as the magnolia trees he stood under.

Fonn began to climb and Thorn followed. The limestone was formed in layered shelves, one above another. Thorn placed his feet on one shelf, then reached up for the one above him.

When they were at the landing in front of the grotto, Thorn followed Fonn inside. It was bright and clean, and lighted through gaping holes in the ceiling, where ferns and moss hung down. The sun poured through the openings, washing shades of green and gold across the white walls. A little brook gurgled and flowed through a shallow basin on the floor of the grotto, then trickled over the edge, down into the pool below.

Thorn turned around and walked back to the edge of the landing, overlooking the valley. He gasped in surprise as he gazed straight out over the tops of giant magnolia trees; shiny green leaves and blooms of pinkish-white flowers filled the air with their fragrance. The real beauty of the trees was often hidden from below, and he had never seen them from above like this.

At that moment a long line of flamingos glided past in front of the cliffs, wingtip to wingtip, just above the tops of the trees. Their long legs trailed behind them, and they were as pink-white as the magnolia blossoms. Thorn felt as if he could reach out and touch them. Over the whisper of the waterfall he heard the twittering cries of cave swallows. Like feathered darts they flew through the curtain of mist, chasing after dancing mayflies. He watched the birds as they dashed back to their nests, each a half-round cup of mud plastered against the wall of the grotto.

Thorn felt a rush of good feeling. He laughed, a joyous, hearty laugh. "This place . . . ," he said, ". . . is different. I wish Nema could see it."

"Then someday she must come with us," said Fonn.

The boy's face lit up. "She would like that. I know she would."

"Now I will show you the great beasts from the past." said Fonn. She laughed. "And you will truly think I am a spirit girl." She balanced herself on the narrow edge of the grotto and led him across to the opposite side, where tall trees shaded the sunlight. She pointed straight down. "Look," she said. "Look deep into the pool and you will see the animals from a long time ago."

· TWELVE

THORN STOOD ON THE HIGH LEDGE. He gazed down into the pool. This time he looked deep into the clear water, past the groupers, past the sharks and other swimming fish. He stared intently, his eyes focused on the bottom, when suddenly he gasped in wonder. Far below, on the sandy floor of the pool, were enormous piles of clean white bones, myriads of them, some piled up, others scattered about in complete disarray. He leaned over the ledge. He could make out great numbers of curved tusks and mounds of heavy leg bones, together with the gigantic skulls of mastodons and mammoths, all strewn randomly over the bottom as if some giant hand had aimlessly tossed them there. None was intact, all were broken.

Fascinated by the strange sight, he lay down on his stomach, his arms outstretched, his head over the side of the ledge, straining his eyes to see more. He recognized the skulls of horses, jaguars and bison, the leg bones of camels and pigs. There were shoulder blades, jawbones and ribs scattered among piles of vertebrae. He saw the bleached white shells of enormous turtles and giant armadillos, some almost as large as the hut he lived in.

"So many animals," he said, pulling himself to his feet. "How did they get here?"

"I do not know," said Fonn. "Maybe they fell in a long time ago and could not get out. Then there were many giant beasts, as many as the birds in the sky and the fish in the waters, maybe even as many as the deer and the bison are today."

Thorn looked again and wondered what it must have been like to see so many living creatures all at one time. He shook his head, puzzled and bewildered. "And Smilodon," he asked, "where is Smilodon?"

Fonn grinned. She removed the sack from her shoulder and placed it on the ledge, then kicked off her sandals. "Wait," she said, "I will show you." She stepped across the ledge at the front of the grotto, to the spot where the water trickled over the edge. She lifted her hands high above her head and poised for a moment. Then with a graceful dive she sprang headfirst down into the pool.

Thorn stepped back, startled. He had not expected this.

Fonn plunged through the water, heading for the bottom. A stream of bubbles followed her down as schools of angelfish and sea perch darted out of her way. She swam easily, her long dark hair streaming out behind her, the shadow of her slim body flowing across the sandy bottom. She moved about here and there, poking among the rubble of bones.

Thorn watched as she turned over some of the huge skulls, reached underneath and picked something up from the sandy floor. One large grouper swam down beside her, snapping at scraps of debris stirred up by her search. Soon many of the parrotfish and even the sharks were following her.

She walks with the animals, thought the boy, now she swims with the fish. If the elders were to see her now, they would be sure she was a spirit girl. He saw a tiny string of bubbles come from her lips, and wondered how she could hold her breath so long.

Then she swam to the other side of the pool, patting the grouper on the snout as she passed. She disappeared behind a pile of bones and Thorn could see her no more.

He waited patiently, knowing that at any moment she must come up, then leaned down to stare into the depths. When she did not appear immediately he grew uneasy. Surely she could not hold her breath so long. More time passed. Do not play games, he thought. He strained his eyes, watching, waiting. Maybe some of the bones had fallen on top of her. Maybe she was trapped. He stopped, then began pacing back and forth along the edge of the grotto, an anxious frown on his face.

Frantically Thorn walked across the ledge, still gazing deep into the pool. He saw a shadow coming up from the bottom. He held his breath. Then he groaned: it was only a grouper.

Finally he hurried down the cliff, jumping reck-lessly from ledge to ledge until he reached the ground. There he leaned down and ran his hand over the green slime that formed a layer around the inner edge of the pool. It was smooth and slippery, and he knew that once you were in the pool there would be no way out.

Thorn got down on his knees. The big groupers were hovering peacefully a little beneath the surface. The sharks cruised lazily, around and around. The reef fish browsed in and out of the jutting rocks and crannies.

Thorn got up quickly. Maybe there was still a chance. Maybe she was trapped under the pile of bones. If he could hold his breath long enough he could reach the bottom. He took a deep breath and stepped back to get a start, but as he was about to jump he heard a voice behind him.

"Clan boy, what is the matter?"

Thorn spun around in shocked surprise. It was Fonn. She stood behind him, dripping wet, holding three long saber teeth in her hand, each longer than a flint knife.

Thorn could hardly believe what he saw. "You are truly a spirit girl," he stammered. "You disappear into the pool, then you walk out of the forest."

For a moment Fonn did not understand. Then she laughed. "I am no spirit," she said. "I swam through an underground stream." She pointed toward the trees. "It flows into another pool, over there, just be-yond the palmettos."

Thorn felt as though he had been fooled again.

"You should have told me before you jumped," he said. "I thought you had drowned."

The girl's laughter died away. "I have been swimming in this pool ever since I was a little child, and I have always come out the same way. I am sorry, I did not think to tell you." She held out three long fangs.

Thorn took the big teeth and turned them over in his hands, quickly forgetting his anger. He ran his thumb along the sharp serrated edges. "The saber fangs of Smilodon," he said.

Fonn said, "The bottom of the pool is covered with them."

Thorn was quiet for a moment, thinking. "Then long ago there were many more Smilodons than there are now?"

"Yes," said Fonn, "and there were many mammoths and mastodons for the big cats to feed on. Now there are few. When they are gone Smilodon will go with them."

"Yet one Smilodon still walks," said Thorn.

"I know," said the girl. "The big cat will hunt far, but he will find little food. If he has seen Long Tusk's calf out on the grasslands, he will remember and will come back."

Thorn smiled. "You speak of things that only a spirit girl would know."

The girl frowned. "I tell you again, clan boy, I am no spirit girl. I have watched the animals and I see how they live." She shrugged. "Maybe I have even come to think as they do."

The next morning, as they made ready to leave, Thorn looked around at the towering tulip trees with their great pink blossoms. "Nema would like it here," he said again.

"And she is welcome," said Fonn, "whenever she is ready."

They went back up through the valley and across the scrub and flatwoods. Shadow perched on Fonn's shoulder. He squawked and cawed and tugged on her ear.

When they came to the bend in the river, Fonn said, "I will stop here." She lifted the crow from her shoulder and tossed him into the air. "Shadow will go with you. When you reach camp give him a twig or a leaf, and he will come back and find me."

As Thorn started off, the girl called after him, "Clan boy, one day soon we will walk with the mastodons."

·THIRTEEN

THE BIG CAT LIMPED BADLY, his slash wounds still festering. The deadly rabies virus had reached his backbone and was multiplying rapidly in the rich juices of his spinal cord. He had gone north fourteen days before, looking for prey that would nourish his aging body. But he no longer had the strength to travel more than a few hours each day.

The gnawing hunger in his belly gave him no rest. He prowled through swamps and thickets but found no game worth taking. He went up into the flatwoods. Turkeys scratching on the pine-needle floor flew away at his approach. Deer and brush pigs scampered off long before he came within sight. He no longer had the dogged tenacity to creep up on his prey. That kind of hunting took energy and patience. Each day now his weight decreased, and he began to feel an unfamiliar pain around the nape of his neck. Now, hunger tearing at his insides, he crept along the riverbank.

FOURTEEN ·

NOT FAR FROM CAMP, Thorn stopped by the river near a clump of ague trees to pick some twigs for Nema. It was growing dark, and as he broke off the fresh green tips he noticed many giant snails laying strings of small, pearl-like eggs on the stems of the water plants. He leaned down, thrust his arm into the water and gathered handfuls of the slow-moving creatures. They were cold and covered with a green scum, and he crammed them into the leather pouch dangling from his belt.

Shadow flew overhead and shouted a warning. But Thorn paid no attention. Caught up in his task, he did not see Smilodon creep into the palmetto shrubs not far away. Now the big cat lay on his belly, his pale yellow eyes watching the boy intently. He moved slowly, silently, ready to pounce.

Thorn stuffed the last of the snails into his leather

pouch. He turned quickly and started up through the loblolly pines, heading for camp.

Smilodon followed, slinking through the palmettos, just out of sight, as if measuring the distance. The rabies virus had almost reached his brain and was dulling his senses. Yet the big cat still possessed enough cunning to circle ahead of the boy and wait for him along the side of the trail. He flattened himself in the darkening shadows of the palmetto fronds and listened. He heard the boy's sandaled feet coming closer. He heard the rattle of the snail shells as they jostled about in the leather pouch.

The boy ran down the slope leading into camp. Smilodon's body stiffened as the sounds came even closer. His muscles quivered and he gathered his legs beneath him and made ready to spring. Closer and closer the dark figure came along the path. The big cat tensed. His pupils widened to focus in the fading light. His ears flicked forward to listen to the pounding, running feet. He waited now. He had killed many mastodon calves and young ground sloths, and once, with his mate, he had brought down an old enfeebled bull mammoth. But he had not yet killed one of these gangly beasts that walked like a bird.

Thorn ran on, holding his spear in front of him, hearing nothing, sensing nothing. His heavy bag of snails swung back and forth, his loose sandals creaked on the bare earth. The boy smiled and hummed to himself as he ran.

Smilodon waited patiently in the middle of the palmetto thicket as the dark figure of the boy grew larger. Closer and closer it came. Now it was directly in front of him. Hunger churned in the big cat's belly. His lower jaw dropped open, gaping wide, freeing the long saber fangs for stabbing. It was time for the kill, finally time to feed.

Suddenly Thorn heard a bleating sound in the underbrush just off the trail. He spun around and saw a young swamp deer standing in the shadows. It would make good bait for his trap. Quickly he jumped after it, hoping to catch it in the tangle of vines.

He chased it around the gum trees. He tripped and stumbled over roots as he hurried after it. He crashed through the thickets, the little animal always just out of reach.

Shadow flew about in dizzy spirals, caught up in the excitement, cawing loudly.

Smilodon came out of hiding and crept up behind them. Silently he waited for his chance to strike. He could still catch glimpses of the boy plunging through the underbrush not far ahead of him, but each time he got into position to spring, the boy disappeared behind a tangle of vines and branches.

Breathlessly, Thorn plunged headlong after the fleeing deer. The little animal squealed in fright as twice Thorn caught it by a hind leg. Each time it pulled free and ran deeper into the thick undergrowth. Then Thorn heard the rustle of leaves as the deer disappeared altogether. He stood for a moment, catching his breath, smiling to himself, almost glad that the little animal had escaped.

He turned slowly and made his way back to the

path, and then started for camp. He had not gone far when he heard a terrified squeal come from the palmetto thicket where he had last seen the little deer. He stopped and listened. The forest was silent, but Thorn knew the little deer had been caught—maybe by a puma or a jaguar. He shrugged and went on his way, and was soon safe within the ring of night fires.

Back in the palmetto thicket Smilodon growled deep in his throat. He had the young swamp deer fast in his jaws. Wearily he carried his small prize down to the river. It would give him strength to go on another day, but it was not enough to satisfy his ravenous hunger.

FIFTEEN ·

AS THORN REACHED HIS HUT he glanced up to see
Shadow still circling overhead. He smiled and held
out an ague twig. The crow flew down, his black
wings brushing against the boy's face as he plucked
the twig from his fingers. Then he flew off and disappeared toward the setting sun.

A few minutes later Thorn sat in the hut with
Nema, eating chunks of roasted snapping-turtle
meat. Together they speared small pieces of the
meat on sharp sticks and held them over the fire,
then dipped them into a stone saucer of fish oil.
Thorn was hungry from his long journey, and he ate
greedily. Next Nema set out a turtle shell full of bit-
tersweet mash made from the pulp of pond apples.

After the meal Nema sat beside the boy, chewing
on a fresh sassafras twig, walking it back and forth
between her lips from one side of her mouth to the
other. She reached over and patted him on the stom-

ach. "The belly is full of meat, the head is full of stories?"

Thorn grinned. This was what he liked best, the long talks they had each time he came home from hunting. There was so much to tell, he hardly knew where to begin. "It is a wide valley, Nema, with tall trees and yellow and orange flowers growing on the big branches. The magnolia trees reach the sky with pink blossoms as thick as the dogwood trees. The air is warm and smells like the sweet oil of pond apples. Black and yellow butterflies fly in the glades, some with purple wings. There are many deer and wood bison in the glades, and ringtail cats climb high in the tulip trees."

Nema sat beside him sewing a broken strap on his sandal with a string of wet gut and a bone needle. She looked sideways at him as she listened, and grinned, her brown teeth worn down, half hidden in the dark cavern of her mouth. She sucked the juice from the twig and stared off into the distance when Thorn finished speaking. Then she said, "Yes, I have heard about it. Long ago our fathers went there, and they came back with shells bigger than my two hands and skins of the jaguar and beautiful feathers of the red ibis."

The boy turned quickly. "You are right, Nema. It is a magical place." The words tumbled out of him. "I saw the grotto and the falls and the deep pool behind the magnolia trees where the flamingos fly. It is different from the grasslands and the scrub. It is even more beautiful than the river that flows behind our camp."

Nema put her needle into a small leather pouch
and wound the long string of gut around her bony
fingers. Then she wrapped pouch and gut together
and tucked them under the tawny pelt on which she
sat. Then she got up and put some dried sassafras
root into the leather sack boiling over the hearth fire.
"It is good to see all those wondrous things."

Thorn jumped up, hardly able to contain himself.
"Then I will take you there, Nema. The spirit girl
can lead us, and you will see where the swallows
nest in the grotto, and where the river runs out of
the stone and splashes over the ledges into the pool.
You can breathe in the smell of the tree flowers and
hear the music of the thrush. We can go and live
there. The spirit girl will have us, I am sure."

Nema chuckled and shook her head. "I would like
to see it. But I am old. How can I walk that far?"

"You would see the bones of animals that lived a
hundred summers ago—mammoths, and turtles
with shells almost as big as this hut."

Nema looked at him sideways, her eyes narrowed.
"Now you talk like a shaman, full of dreams and vi-
sions."

Thorn held out his hands. "No, Nema, I tell the
truth. It is a deep pool, and on the bottom are huge
bones and tusks of the thunder beasts and mastodons and all the other giant animals that once
came there to drink. They lie in great piles across
the sandy bottom."

Nema chewed on her twig, thinking. Then her eyes
lit up. "Maybe so—even when I was a girl, the long-
necks wandered over the grasslands, and thunder

beasts and giant ground sloths were many."

They sat for a long while talking. Finally Thorn got up. He put some of the large snails into an empty turtle shell. "I must give these to the shaman. I will let him know what I have seen."

Nema grunted. "He told you not to walk with the girl. It will be like talking to an angry scrub jay."

"I know," said Thorn, "but the things I have to tell are good. Maybe he will change his mind."

SIXTEEN ·

A SOFT BREEZE WHISPERED through the palm trees and Thorn heard the *pit-pit* of a nighthawk. He stood in front of the shaman's hut and held out the turtle shell full of snails. "Great leader," he called out, "keeper of the spirits, I bring you more gifts from the river."

Thorn waited. He heard sounds of feet shuffling inside the hut, and saw light as a fish-oil lamp was lit. Then Dour's voice came in answer. "What manner of fish do you bring?"

"No fish," Thorn answered. "Fresh pond snails as big as my fist." Thorn chuckled to himself; he knew the snails were not quite that large.

"Good," cried Dour. "The spirits accept your gifts. Remove your sandals and enter."

Thorn kicked off his sandals. He stooped over and pushed his way past the heavy mammoth hide across the doorway.

The shaman sat on the stump of a palm log toward the back of the hut, surrounded by jaguar pelts and egret plumes. A skirt of spotted deerskin was wrapped tightly around his waist, tied with a strip of alligator hide. His shallow chest was bare and unpainted. He peered through the dim light as if he could not see very well. "Eh, clan boy, there you are. Lay down your gifts."

Thorn placed the turtle shell on the ground in front of the shaman, then stepped back a respectful distance.

"Speak," said the old man.

Thorn cleared his throat and swallowed hard. "I walked with the spirit girl."

"Hrump," said Dour, his tiny eyes hard and narrow. "You think I did not know?"

"Huh?" Thorn grunted.

"One of the hunters saw you down by the river."

Thorn stiffened. "Did he also follow us to the land of the Lake Dwellers?"

Dour's mouth dropped open. "You went that far?"

"A journey of two days," said Thorn.

"And you found the land dry and empty?"

Thorn frowned. "No . . . no, it was not empty. There was much game. The streams flowed with many fish, and the trees were full of fruits and flowers." He went on describing all the things he had seen, the flamingos, the eagle rays and the pool of bones. He told how he and Fonn had met the cave bear and how they had saved the giant ground sloth from the dire wolves.

The old man placed his withered hands over his nose and mouth as if in prayer, and listened. His eyes hardened again and he interrupted. "I think you are wrong," he said. "Many times I have seen the signs in my sleep. The land of the Lake Dwellers is always dark and evil. Vultures roost in the dead trees and huge black cats prowl the night."

"I—I saw nothing like that, nothing."

"Then maybe you were under a spell. Maybe you saw only what the spirit girl wanted you to see."

Thorn hesitated. At first he didn't know what to say. Then he blurted out, "My story is true. The things I saw, the things that happened were as real as my eyes, my ears, my hands. I saw them, I heard them, I felt them. Even if I tried to make them up I could not think of such things."

The shaman busied himself with the dried head of a lizard, turning it this way and that, reading the signs. "And the girl," he asked, "what about the girl?"

Thorn shook his head in frustration. "She is only a girl, as I am only a boy, nothing more."

"No, no, no," snapped Dour. "What is she like? What kind of weapons does she carry?"

"No weapons," said Thorn.

"Nothing?"

"Only a knife made from the fang of a sabertooth," said Thorn.

The old man's eyes widened. "Ah, from the tooth of Smilodon."

Thorn shrugged.

"And what else?"

"I told you," said Thorn. "The girl knows the animals well."

The old man's eyes closed until they were narrow slits. "I believe you," he said. "You tell me the girl can do all these things, but you do not think she is a spirit girl?"

Thorn swallowed hard. He felt his hands begin to tremble. "No," he said bluntly, "she is not. Nor can she cast a spell."

"Then your eyes deceive you," said the old man. "For you have told me the cave bear fled from her shadow. You were surrounded by wolves, and the girl raised her hand and the wolves disappeared. Do you know any hunter who can do such things?"

Thorn folded his arms across his chest and bit his lip. The shaman was mixing everything up, twisting his stories around so that they seemed evil. "It is only that she knows how the animals think."

Dour looked up quickly, a thin smirk on his wrinkled face. "Now, at last, you speak the truth. She kills with the tooth of Smilodon and she thinks like a beast."

The boy grimaced. He did not wish to listen to such talk. "She is only as you and I," he said. "She is no different."

"Huh, you believe that?"

"Yes."

"Then you are a fool." The shaman walked across the small hut, mumbling to himself. Then he turned slowly and pointed a bony finger in the boy's face. "I told you once before she is a changeling. She is the spirit of Smilodon."

"I cannot believe that."

"So tell me, have you ever seen her and Smilodon at the same time? Have you stood beside her and heard the beast roar in another part of the forest?"

The boy licked his lips. He could think of no instance when he had seen Fonn and heard the cat roar at the same time. "I—"

"Well?"

Thorn shook his head.

"And you never will," said Dour. "Because she and Smilodon are the same. You will never see them apart. There are times when she walks as a spirit girl and times when she prowls like a cat."

This was madness, beyond belief. "The spirit girl, the ghost of Smilodon? Never." Thorn mumbled the words under his breath.

But the old man heard him. "One and the same," he said.

"I only know she has done no wrong," said Thorn. "She lives her own way and she harms no one."

Dour was still pacing, still talking to himself, putting the pieces of the mystery together in his mind. Then he stopped and looked down at Thorn. "Four summers ago I was there when Nema skinned the evil cat. She plunged the knife into the chest. I heard the hissing breath escape from the body. That was the spirit of Smilodon. At that moment the spirit girl came forth."

Thorn cringed. The whole thing was like a demon story told by the elders.

Dour looked down at him once more. "Your father was killed by Smilodon. If you continue to befriend the girl, your fate will be the same."

Thorn wanted to hear no more. As soon as the shaman finished talking, the boy turned and went out into the night. Barred owls hooted in the loblolly pines and a puma cried out. Thorn walked across the clearing in the center of the camp, his mind denying all the foolish things he had just heard. I do not believe any of it, he told himself.

He smiled and remembered Fonn's words: the shaman sees things that are not there, he hears voices that do not speak.

SEVENTEEN ·

THE NEXT DAY WAS CLEAR, the air along the riverbank heavy with the fragrance of blue flag and pickerel weed. A bright morning sun bathed the land in a golden glow, and thick white clouds hung in the blue sky. To Thorn they looked like great puffy fish floating slowly in the warm air.

He dropped his spear on the riverbank, took off his sandals, tied the leather straps together and slung them around his neck. Then he stepped into the warm, rippling waters searching for stones, smooth round stones that could be used for throwing. When he found one that he liked he picked it up, shook off the water and put it into the leather pouch hanging from his belt. As soon as he had enough he would go up into the scrub and pine wood. There, if he was lucky, and his aim was good, he would kill a turkey or some sand grouse for Nema.

He waded up and down the stream, leaning over,

staring into the water. All at once a small olive-shaped bean hit him on the head. He glanced up and another one struck him on the chest. The gum tree sheds its fruit early, he thought. He took another step. This time he heard a low guttural growl. He stumbled backward and looked up into the branches. Just over his head, in the speckled canopy of fluttering leaves, he could make out a slender form draped across the branches. He turned quickly and splashed through the shallow water, racing for the bank to get his spear. He reached for it, spun around and waited tensely for what he thought would be a hungry puma or a small jaguar.

Then he heard a high-pitched giggle. He stood there for a moment, puzzled and uncertain.

Suddenly Fonn dropped out of the tree and landed in the shallow water as lightly as an egret. She held her sides laughing and tried to catch her breath, her dark shiny hair hanging down over her shoulders.

Thorn bristled in anger. Once again the girl had caught him off guard, once again he felt like a little boy. He watched as she waded toward him, still giggling. He gritted his teeth and pressed his lips together to control his temper. She is like her stupid crow, he thought, always laughing.

Fonn carried her sandals tied around her neck, as he did, and she had a leather sack slung over her shoulder. She smiled brightly. "The day is good," she said, and glanced up at the sky. "The shadows of the clouds will bring the beasts out onto the grasslands. Today we can walk with the mastodons."

Thorn quickly forgot his anger. This is what he had been hoping for. He had never been close to a live mastodon. The turkeys and sand grouse would have to wait. He sat on the bank and tied on his sandals. Then he picked up his spear. "I am ready," he said.

The girl shook her head. "Your spear—lay it down. Today you are not a hunter."

He looked at her, then shrugged and went to hide his spear in a clump of palmettos. He turned back, smiling. "Now I am ready."

Side by side they ran across the sandy scrub. Shadow flew over their heads, cawing, circling above as if leading them on. From time to time he flew down and perched on Fonn's shoulder.

Soon they came to the open grasslands, which stretched far off into the distance, in endless vistas of golden savanna. Isolated hammocks of cabbage palms and magnolias stood out like sentinels in a waving sea of grass.

Fonn led the way as they pushed through the knee-high grass. They ran near a burrowing owl sitting on its mound of earth. It bobbed up and down and watched them closely, then ducked into its hole as they went by.

Far out on the savanna they came to a single palm tree. It was surrounded by palmetto bushes and curved high into the sky. The clan people called it the lone palm. Because of its bowlike shape it was easy to climb.

Fonn stopped beneath it and held up her hand.

"Wait. I will see if the mastodons are out in the open yet."

Thorn watched as she kicked off her sandals and went up the slanting palm. She climbed hand over hand, her bare feet curving around the rough gray trunk. Thorn followed right behind her. She climbs like an ocelot, he thought. When she reached the top she looked out over the savanna, searching the horizon from one side to the other. With her arms wrapped around the tree trunk she glanced down and shook her head.

The boy groaned in disappointment. There were no mastodons. They would have to wait for another day. He slid to the ground as she started to come down. Suddenly he saw her body stiffen as if she had seen something new. Quickly she climbed back up and put one hand to her forehead, shielding her eyes against the sun. Again and again she squinted toward the east. Then she looked down. This time she grinned.

"They are there," she shouted, "feeding on the gumbo trees close to the big hammock."

Thorn felt his heart leap. "How many?"

"Three cows." Fonn looked again. "And a young one."

"Maybe Long Tusk is one of them," said Thorn.

The girl slid down from her high perch and nodded. "Come," she said. "They are still far away, but we must be careful not to scare them off."

It was difficult to see any great distance, so they stopped every few moments to look over the top of the high grass and be sure they were heading in the right direction. The dry grass rustled softly beneath the boy's feet, and he smelled the warm sweetness of the savanna.

Fonn pointed to a distant group of palms and mahogany trees in the middle of the savanna. She spoke softly. "We must head for the big hammock. The mastodons will stay close to the trees for safety."

At first the trees appeared to be close, but as he pushed his way through the tall grass and the long moments dragged on, Thorn became impatient. It seemed that they would never get there. By standing on his toes he could just begin to make out what appeared to be grayish-brown hillocks moving aimlessly about. They were the mastodons, browsing slowly from one bush to another. His pulse raced. He had seen mastodons before, but he had never been able to get this close to the giant beasts.

Fonn stopped. She reached out and pulled a handful of dry straw and seeds from a grass stem, crumbled them in her fist, then held them up and let the dust sprinkle out of her hand. It blew away on the gentle breeze. "Good," said Fonn. "The wind is coming toward us."

She started out again, walking slowly, leading Thorn on a path that would bring them directly in front of the browsing mastodons.

Thorn stood on his toes. Now he could see them clearly, huge, grayish boulderlike shapes, moving slowly. Two of the cows were off to one side. The other one was with the calf.

"It is Long Tusk," said Fonn. "I walked with her many days ago, before she had her calf. Now she will be more cautious." With that the girl began walking about, head down, searching for something on the ground.

"What do you look for?" asked Thorn.

"Dung," said the girl, "mastodon droppings."

Thorn began looking too. It wasn't long before he found a clump of old dung beside a palmetto bush. "Here," he said.

Fonn reached down and picked up one of the dried chips. She rubbed it over her arms and legs.

Thorn looked at her, puzzled. "What are you doing?"

She grinned. "Come," she said, "you must do the same. It takes away the man smell."

Grudgingly Thorn picked up a small piece of the sun-baked droppings and began rubbing it lightly over his arms.

Fonn wrinkled her nose. Her voice choked as she tried to stifle a giggle. "Now you smell like an old bull," she whispered.

They went on again, slowly, one step at a time. Fonn lifted her arm high and turned her hand back and forth; at the same time she made low rumbling sounds deep in her throat.

Instantly the big elephantlike beasts stopped feeding. They turned and looked in the direction of the boy and girl. Long snakelike trunks went up, sniffing, searching the air.

Fonn stopped and Thorn waited a short distance behind her.

The huge beasts watched them intently. Their trunks continued to sweep back and forth over the tall grass, testing the air, trying to size up the intruders. They were tense, uncertain, ready to flee at any moment.

Slowly Fonn moved ahead, grumbling softly in her throat, waving her right hand over her head. The boy followed close behind her until they were only a hundred paces from the giant beasts. There they stopped again.

Thorn held his breath. He stood quietly, his heart pounding. They are not as tall as mammoths, he thought, but they are massive and powerful. He marveled at their long curved ivory tusks, their small ears and scraggly coats of sparse gray hair.

The animals stared back at Thorn, unsettled and cautious; their tiny eyes squinted in the bright sunlight. Flocks of cowbirds perched on and climbed across their leathery backs, feeding on the ticks and flies that swarmed around the massive beasts.

Gently Fonn lifted Shadow from her shoulder and tossed him into the air. The noisy crow flew up and circled around the big animals, calling *ca-ha, ca-ha, ca-ha.* He flew in front of their faces, then landed on Long Tusk's back.

"Long Tusk will feel safe now," Fonn whispered. "She is used to Shadow. When the birds quiet down, she knows there is no danger."

Thorn followed the girl as they moved near, stepping carefully through the waist-high grass. It crackled beneath their sandaled feet.

Fonn held her hand up higher, turning it as if it

were a trunk. She kept up the low rumbling sound as she walked closer.

Thorn felt a giddiness in the pit of his stomach. The beasts towered in front of him like huge boulders. With tiny eyes they studied him closely, their long ivory tusks, sharp and deadly, pointed at his chest.

"Come," Fonn whispered.

Cautiously the boy took a step closer. Suddenly the cowbirds flew up in a mass and circled around like a small black cloud of beating wings. They swooped, turned and dived over the heads of the boy and girl, the sound of their wings like the patter of rain on leaves. Once, twice, three times they circled. Then they flew back and settled down again on the broad backs of the mastodons.

Beads of sweat formed on Thorn's forehead as the giant beasts eyed him closely.

"They are used to me now," Fonn whispered. "But they may come closer to touch you. Do not run." She walked forward quietly, slowly, still making grumbling noises in her throat and turning her upraised hand back and forth.

The mastodons seemed uneasy and Thorn waited tensely, wondering if the big cow would charge. Yet Fonn stepped even closer, almost within reach of Long Tusk's waving trunk.

Then the little calf squealed and the mother mastodon lowered her head and came forward, answering Fonn in the same low rumbling sounds. She threw up her trunk and blew a shower of grass and dirt into the air. The little calf backed away and hid behind its mother.

Fonn stayed where she was, her right hand high over her head. With her left she reached into the leather pouch slung over her shoulder. She took out a long brownish-green papaw and held it out in her fingers to the calf. "Come, little one," she said quietly. "This is for you."

The calf made squeaking sounds and pressed against its mother's flank, peering out with suspicion at this strange creature.

Fonn continued talking in a quiet voice, all the while holding up the tempting fruit. The small calf came cautiously from behind its mother. It hobbled toward Fonn, its legs shuffling through the dry grass, then stopped a short distance away and stretched out its little trunk as far as it would go. Gently it picked the fruit from her fingers. Then it turned and with a tiny squeak ran back and hid behind its mother.

Fonn held out another papaw. This time Long Tusk stepped closer, nudging the calf ahead of her with her trunk. The little calf became bolder. It waddled up timidly and took the fruit from the girl's fingers and put it in its mouth. While it chewed on the soft pod it explored the girl's face, arms and hands with its supple trunk. Suddenly the calf discovered the leather pouch full of fruit and squealed with delight. It reached into the bag and took out one papaw after another, stuffing its mouth until the pouch was empty. With low slobbering sounds the animal chewed greedily, and strings of yellow juice dripped from its lips.

Now the cow came closer. She touched the girl's face with the tip of her trunk. Fonn stood still and talked to the animal in a low rumble as she reached up and gently patted it on the trunk.

Thorn's fists clenched tight at his sides. He had never seen anything like it. Long Tusk was only a hand's length away from the girl. With one step the huge beast could crush her like a dried oak leaf. Then his heart jumped as the other two cows began moving toward him.

Fonn turned slowly. "Do not run," she whispered. "They will not harm you."

Thorn stood quietly, listening to the blood pounding in his ears as the huge animals loomed over him. Their tiny eyes studied him intently for a moment. One of them scooped up a trunkful of dust and grass and tossed it over its back. Then both cows came forward and stroked him on the chest and shoulders with the tips of their trunks, their touch so gentle he felt as if palm leaves were brushing across his body.

Their curiosity satisfied, the big cows backed off. They had begun browsing in branches of nearby gumbo trees, when the cowbirds flew up. Shadow followed them, cawing. The mastodons lifted their trunks and began sniffing the air. They crowded together, touching each other, keeping the little one between them, then they backed away, turned and disappeared into the safety of the nearby hammock.

"They are frightened," said Thorn. "Why?"

The girl looked around quickly. She sniffed the air. "I don't know," she said, "but they smell danger."

Thorn felt uneasy. Out in the open, without a spear, he felt naked and vulnerable. He glanced up and saw a giant condor in the sky, then another and another. They soared in tight circles, moving slowly, following something on the ground.

The girl looked up too. She grimaced. "Smilodon. The vultures follow and wait for a kill."

A chill ran through Thorn's body. The peaceful days of roaming the grasslands were over. The evil cat was back.

·EIGHTEEN

SMILODON LAY HIDDEN IN the yellow grass of the savanna, his great head resting on his paws. Hunger churned in his belly and from time to time he looked up and watched the gangly beasts that walked on two legs like birds. He saw them cutting wood along the edge of their camp, and he waited for one of them to come out close enough for him to pounce on. None did. And so he waited, his eyes watering as the nagging pain in the nape of his neck throbbed. By night he prowled outside the ring of fires, barred from entry by the hated flames, roaring his frustrations to the stars.

NINETEEN ·

AFTER THORN LEFT THE GIRL down by the river, he rushed back to camp and went directly to the hut of the flintmaker. Inside, the air was heavy and warm; the big puma and llama pelts that normally covered the entrance were thrown back to let in a breath of air and a patch of sunlight.

Oom was hunched over the big skull that served as his workbench. With a flint graver he was cutting out long, sharp needles from the antler of a deer.

Thorn stood before him, panting. He did not even wait to catch his breath before he blurted out, "Smilodon is back."

The young man looked up quickly. "I have been expecting him."

"You knew?"

Oom nodded. "I know he still looks for me."

Thorn wanted to tell him that the cat was no ghost, but he knew it would do no good. Instead he

said, "So I will dig a deep pit—plant the great spear
in the middle. The cat will fall in and impale himself
on it and die."

"Good," said Oom, "I have talked with the shaman. If the evil cat dies by its own doing, the omen
will be fulfilled."

Thorn's face brightened. He slapped his thigh.
"Then you agree?"

Oom's white teeth flashed in a grin. "The cat may
be a ghost, boy, but he is not beyond death." He held
up a tight fist in a gesture of determination. "Tomorrow morning, when the sun is high, we will make
the great spear."

Thorn grinned. This was the Oom he knew.

That night Thorn lay on the big tawny pelt in
Nema's hut. He slept fitfully, running his fingers
through the soft fur. His hand reached up to the
huge head. His fingertips touched the hard black
lips. Then he heard the deep-throated roar, thundering out over the grasslands, shaking the very earth.

The next morning the boy got up early. He made
his way across the clearing of the little camp, past
the women at the cook fires. He smelled the honey-
sweet odor of water-bean cakes baking on the flat
hearthstones. They were tempting, but this morning
he had more important things on his mind.

In Oom's hut he sat on a palm log beside the big
skull while the flintmaker lifted the skin flap of the
hut and removed some of the palmetto branches to
let in more light. Oom hummed as he laid out his
stone tools. His eyes were somber but he looked at
Thorn with a wide grin.

From a skin sack at the rear of the hut he took out a large chunk of stone. It was the size of a man's head and was partially covered with chalk.

He turned it around in his hand, showing it to Thorn. "The flint core you brought in last summer. I have saved it for a time like this."

Thorn smiled. "It was buried in the sand, near the limestone spring—the biggest one I have ever found."

Oom nodded and placed the stone on top of the big skull. Then he sat down to begin his work. His right arm was stiff from the long scar, and it moved awkwardly, but his hand was still good; he could hold things firmly. With a sharp bone tool he scraped away the chalk from the stone until he exposed the greenish-black flint within. Then he leaned over and pressed his ear against it, and tapped it with a small stone. He listened again and smiled his approval. "The flint is good," he said. "It will cleave well."

Next he held it up, turning it in the bright light, studying it intently. He grunted and tapped it lightly with his finger.

Thorn sat on the edge of his seat. "You look for a long time," he said. "What do you see?"

"I see the heart of the stone within," said Oom. "I must strike around it carefully, to cut away everything that is not needed to shape out the great spearhead."

"So it will be just right?" said Thorn.

Oom grunted. "If I strike in the wrong place the entire flint may be wasted." He glanced around the hut, his eyes moving over the dusty piles of bones, the slabs of limestone and the small tusks of ivory. He shook his head. "I do not think I have another one large enough for the task."

Thorn winced and folded his arms across his chest to ease the suspense.

Now the young weaponmaker picked up a stone hammer. He began striking the flint, chipping off sharp flakes, most of which fell to the floor. He continued working, turning the flint stone around and around. Slowly it began to glisten clean and bright, with crystalline shades of green, ebony black and yellow.

Oom bent over his work with quiet, deliberate movements, almost forgetting Thorn was there. Little by little a crude spearhead began to emerge from the rough stone. Oom smiled. "There now, it begins to live."

He placed a soft pelt apron on his lap and held the piece firmly between his knees. With his right hand he picked up a sharp boar tusk and pressed it against the glossy stone. Then he punched the tusk with the heel of his left hand. A thin sliver of flint flaked off and fell onto the apron. He repeated the process, tapping and chipping around the entire stone. He held it up once again, studied it thoughtfully, turned it this way and that.

Thorn looked on in fascination. Sweat beaded his forehead and he wiped it away with the back of his hand. He followed every move of the flintmaker as if he were watching the work of a magician.

Now, using a tine from a deer antler, Oom pressed off tiny fragments all along the cutting edge of the point. He felt more relaxed as he applied the finishing touches: the tense moments were past.

Without looking up from his work he said, "So you saw Smilodon?"

Thorn was startled by the sudden question. "Well, no." He shook his head. "I did not see him."

"But you heard him roar?"

"Yes, he came back last night, just as the spirit girl said he would."

Oom looked up quickly, his eyes narrowed. "I wonder how she would know that."

"She listens and watches," said Thorn. "She can tell when the animals are frightened. She knows how they think."

"Perhaps she knows because she is a changeling."

The boy frowned. "Dour said that."

"Yes," said Oom. "It is true. You never saw the girl and the cat at the same time, you never heard the roar while the girl was standing beside you."

Thorn groaned. "I do not care. The shaman says the spirits tell him this. I think it is false. She is like us—no different."

Oom looked up, a half-smile on his handsome bronze face. "You do not think much of the spirits, do you?"

"I am not sure about such things," the boy said. "But I know the girl is not one of them."

Oom's long fingers continued chipping and shaping the spearhead as he talked. "It is good you have a friend to hunt with," he said. "But be careful. The girl may be a demon we do not understand."

Thorn bristled. Oom is getting to be like Dour, the boy thought, he hangs onto a foolish notion like a snapping turtle hangs onto a garfish. "She is a friend," he said. "I know she harms no living thing. Someday the shaman and the clan people will know that too."

Oom nodded and went on with his work. Before long the new spearhead glistened, sharp and shiny as a piece of fractured glass. The flintmaker carved out a wide groove on each side of the head, a place on which to bind the shaft. He examined it with pride, then held it out to the boy.

Thorn took it in his hand, held it up to the light and ran his fingertips over its hard rippling surface. He laid it flat on his open palm. It was almost as large as his hand. His eyes widened with satisfaction. "It is good, Oom. Like an amulet or a magic stone."

"It is that way with many things," said Oom. "Beauty can hide a deadly purpose." He reached into the jaws of the big skull and brought up a small parcel of moleskin. He unfolded it carefully and took out a delicate flint spearhead, and handed it to the boy. "This is a willow leaf," he said. "It too is beautiful. It too is made to kill."

Thorn was amazed. He had never seen such a magnificent spearhead before. It was long, thin and narrow, and shaped exactly like a willow leaf. He held it up to the light. It was transparent as amber, and the rays of the sun shone through it like sparkling points of fire. He ran his fingers along the edges and winced as the sharp point pricked his thumb. A small trickle of blood oozed out and ran down into his palm. Quickly he handed the spearhead back and squeezed his thumb in his fist to stop the bleeding.

Oom smiled. "It cuts like the tooth of Smilodon," he said. "But it is not for hunting."

"Yet you say it is made for killing?" Thorn asked, still nursing his thumb.

"Yes," said Oom. "It has been blessed with special powers by the shaman. Once it leaves the hand it goes straight to its mark. It cannot miss."

"And it is not for animals?"

"No," said Oom. "It is to be used only against the evil spirits."

The flintmaker rolled the willow leaf up in the soft pelt and placed it back in the skull. Then he picked up the great spearhead. "Now you must go out into the forest and cut down a strong sapling as long as your shadow. We will bind it to the spearhead and our great spear will be ready."

Thorn did as he was told. In the forest he found a strong young gum tree, straight as a shaft of sunlight. He cut it down and with his flint knife trimmed the branches and shaved away the bark until he had a sturdy pole, twice his height and as thick as his arm. He brought it back to Oom.

The flintmaker split one end of the pole, then jammed the great spearhead in place and bound it tightly with wet deer sinew. Then he limped to a small hearth fire and held the spear over the heat, turning it slowly until the binding dried tight and firm.

Thorn looked at it, admired its sturdiness and strength. "It is the biggest spear I have ever seen," he said. "But it is not for throwing."

"No," said Oom, "it is much too heavy for that. Now you must plant it in the center of your trap, out on the grasslands. Then we will wait for Smilodon to come."

TWENTY ·

THORN DUG HIS TRAP OUT on the grasslands, close to the lone palm tree. The shaman ordered two clan women to help him, and with large snapping-turtle shells they dug a deep hole in the sandy loam, two spears long and one and one-half spears wide. All day they dug, deeper and deeper, laboring under the hot sun as the sweat ran down their backs and faces.

The next day Thorn went into the pit and handed shellfuls of sand and dirt up to the women to scatter across the grasslands. When the pit opening was above his head, he planted the great spear firmly in the center, its sharp tip pointing to the sky. Around it, he placed long spikes of ironwood.

With the women he cut long poles from nearby sumac trees and crisscrossed them over the hole from edge to edge. These they covered lightly with palmetto fronds, then sprinkled with a layer of dried grass.

When the trap was finished, Thorn went down to the backwater swamps and speared a string of bowfin and garfish. He placed them carefully in the center of the trap on top of the leaves and grass. Now, tempted by the smell of fish broiling in the hot sun, Smilodon would come. When he stepped onto the flimsy covering of branches to get at the bait he would fall through and impale himself on the sharp spear.

The next morning dawned hot and dry. The sky was a cloudless, arid blue. All day long the dead fish baked in the bright sun, fermenting until the fulsome odor drifted far out across the savanna.

Each night the clan people heard the big cat roar and each day Thorn climbed to the top of the lone palm tree to look out over the grasslands and wait for Smilodon. Thorn knew that if the cat were hungry enough he would come. Two days passed, then three, and still the big cat did not show up.

Thorn kept his daily vigil, and as the pungent smell became stronger, swarms of blowflies gathered around the odorous trap. Carrion beetles too were attracted by the odor, and twice Thorn had to climb down from his lookout to chase off persistent black bears that came to steal the bait.

Then one morning the clan people awoke to find Smilodon's pug marks in the middle of the camp. They ran about in panic: the cat must have come brazenly through the night fires into the very center of the clearing.

Oom was shaken. He limped out to the trap with

Thorn and kicked sand at the covering of branches. "It's no use," he stormed. "Smilodon looks not for smoldering fish. He looks for me. The seven families in this clan may die if I do not. The omen will not pass until I meet him face to face." His eyes narrowed as he stared out across the grasslands.

Thorn saw the madness in the young man's eyes. He tugged at Oom's belt. "Wait a little longer," he pleaded. "I will get fresh bait, a tapir, a swamp deer. Then he will come, you will see."

Oom shrugged the boy off. "I will promise nothing."

Without waiting to hear more, Thorn went down to the riverbank. He carried his spear in his hand and a spear thrower under his belt. He walked quietly, smelling the fragrant pickerelweed that grew along the muddy bank. After making his way through a stand of tall sawgrass, he came to a narrow sandbar and followed it silently until he found what he was looking for: river hogs, two of them, fat and sleepy, basking in the warm sunlight.

Carefully Thorn removed the spear thrower from his belt. The short, sticklike implement was fashioned from a deer antler; with it a spear could be thrown far and with greater force and accuracy. Slowly, very slowly, Thorn placed the shaft of his spear into the notch on the end of the thrower. He lifted the spear over his head, his right hand gripping the thrower, his left aiming the spear. He stood for a moment and held his breath.

The animal nearest him raised its head and looked

around, sniffing, sensing danger. Thorn waited no longer. He threw the spear with all his might. It pierced the hog deep through the heart. The animal jumped and let out a high-pitched squeal. It struggled for an instant, then rolled over on its side, dead. The other beast leaped into the river and disappeared.

Thorn was pleased. Now he had bait that would attract the vultures, and the vultures would guide Smilodon to the trap. He threw the little hog over his shoulder and hurried back to camp. First he went to Oom's hut to show him the new bait. But the young flintmaker was not there. Thorn ran to Nema's hut and found her sitting on the bare earth. The big Smilodon pelt was gone.

When she saw the boy, Nema threw up her hands. "He is mad," she said. "He is possessed of demons."

Thorn jumped in front of her. "Who is mad, Nema?"

"Oom is mad. He came in crazy as a scrub jay and pulled the hide up from the floor. He said Smilodon was looking for his skin. He rolled it up under his arm and ran out, shouting, 'Death to the evil cat!'"

Thorn leaned down and looked into her face. "Where did he go, Nema?"

"Where? Where would the madman go? Out to find Smilodon."

Thorn raced across the clearing. He saw Ute sitting on the path that led to the savanna. She held her head in her hands and sobbed, a bowl of hackberries still in her lap.

Thorn knelt beside her. "Where did he go, Ute?"

The girl looked up, her eyes wet. "Out on the grasslands," she said. "I could not stop him. He said if he did not do this, I would die and Nema would die."

Thorn waited to hear no more. With the river hog bouncing on his shoulder he raced across the savanna. Far off on the horizon he saw the lone palm tree slanting against the sky. He hurried toward it, pushing his way through the waist-high grass. As he approached the trap, he saw that it had been uncovered and the great spear was gone. Without stopping he hurried on. Then, in the distance he heard Oom's voice shouting a wild challenge to the spirits.

The boy ran toward it. He found the flintmaker sitting cross-legged under the lone palm tree. Perspiration beaded his face and chest, and his bronze skin glistened in the sunlight. A headband of ocelot skin circled his dark hair. The big pelt was spread out beneath him. He pointed the great spear at an angle in front of him, holding the blunt end firmly against the ground, shouting his protest to the winds. "Ayah, evil cat, I crouch upon your back! I spit upon your ghostly hide! Come! Let me see your wrath! Throw yourself upon my spear."

Thorn ran up to him, panting heavily. "Oom," he shouted, "if the cat comes he will kill you."

"Or I him," said Oom. "Either way the omen will be fulfilled."

The boy shook his head. He held up the hog. Blood dripped from it and ran down his arm. "Look, I have new bait. The vultures will see it and lead Smilodon to the trap. Come, let us set it again. Then there will be no danger."

"No," said Oom, "we cannot wait. The beast grows bolder." The flintmaker grinned, and the boy saw a strange happiness in his dark eyes, as if he welcomed this ghostly duel. "This way is better," said Oom. "Now I am his bait."

"But it is not a spirit," said Thorn. He felt anger building up within him. "It is a thing of flesh and blood and—"

Oom held up his hand. "Silence, clan boy."

Thorn dropped his spear and the river hog to the ground. He heard a rustling in the tall grass. "Oom, leave—leave now before it is too late."

Oom cocked his head to one side and listened. "I will kill him," he shouted. "I will kill him, or he will kill me." He threw back his head and laughed like a wild man.

Thorn pulled at Oom's arm, but the young man did not budge. His eyes were glassy and he stared ahead, holding his spear steady in one hand, making a fist with the other.

Thorn gazed out over the savanna. He could see nothing but the waves of golden grass. Then he glanced up at the slanting palm tree, kicked off his sandals and started to climb. He grasped the trunk with his palms and fingers and went up hand over hand, climbing with his bare feet as if he were going up a rocky ledge. When he reached the top he looked out, far over the savanna. He searched the length of the horizon, looking for the cat.

Far below, the mad flintmaker continued to shout his ghostly challenge.

Thorn could see nothing but the endless waves of grass. Then he noticed a big armadillo rooting for grubs beside a tall palmetto shrub not far away. That must have been what Oom heard, he thought.

Thorn gazed out again but saw nothing unusual. He had started to climb down when he saw a giant condor circling in the distance. Soon other vultures joined it, all soaring in tight circles. Once more he looked out over the grasslands. A band of chestnut-colored horses galloped off to the west, followed by small groups of llamas. Thorn held on to his perch.

He stared into the distance. Flocks of white egrets flew up along the horizon. Far out, Thorn was sure he saw the grass parting. Something was coming. His heart leaped as a huge, tawny head rose up above the grass. He shook his head and looked again. It was the big cat. He came through the tall grass, holding his head high, his ears cocked forward, listening. He had heard Oom's call and was coming to answer the challenge.

It was the first time Thorn had seen the big cat alive. He was a giant. His huge head reached as high as a man's shoulders. Enormous fangs, white, curved like two long daggers, jutted down from either side of his upper jaw.

Thorn held his breath as he watched the great beast creep up slowly, deliberately stalking. He limped on his left side and he seemed to sway, as if unsteady on his feet. He did not sniff the ground but stopped from time to time and lifted his head high, searching the savanna.

Once again Oom shouted his challenge. The big cat turned his head and listened. Then he came on, boldly, heading straight for the mad flintmaker.

Thorn wrapped his arms around the trunk of the palm tree and hung on. "Oom," he whispered. "Oom! The beast!" His heart was beating fast. With his bad arm Oom could not climb, but he could run. Thorn's fingers pressed into the hard gray bark. "Oom!" he said out loud. But the young hunter seemed not to hear.

The huge beast came on in a steady pace, again attracted by the wild shouts. Now Thorn could see the great shoulders, the heavy muscles rippling beneath the tawny hide. He saw the cold yellow eyes staring straight ahead and heard the deep guttural growl from Smilodon's throat.

Thorn leaned forward against the trunk of the tree and closed his eyes. He listened. All he could hear was the pulse of his own blood pounding in his ears. There was no angry growl, no scream, no sound of violence.

He waited. Long moments went by. He shook his head. Surely it must have happened. Thorn opened his eyes and looked down. He could hardly believe what he saw. Oom was still sitting there, quietly now, rocking back and forth, waiting for the cat to come and impale himself on the great spear.

Once again the boy looked out over the grasslands. The cat was gone. Thorn searched back and forth carefully. Then, off to one side, he saw the tawny body, blending in with the yellow grass. The cat had changed direction. He hunched low, slinking through the tall grass, every few moments lifting his head and staring off into the distance. He was now stalking a new victim.

Thorn followed Smilodon's gaze and saw the reason for his change of interest. It was Long Tusk, the mastodon cow. She had come out in the cool shadows of the afternoon with her calf. She was away from the small herd, away from the safety of the distant hammock, unaware that her calf was in danger.

· TWENTY-ONE

THE BIG CAT LAY IN THE TALL grass, eyeing the mastodon and her calf. He felt a stiffness in his limbs and a sharp stabbing pain in his ribs when he breathed. The flesh wound on his shoulder was still unhealed and the one on his flank was festering badly where the bat had tapped it. The deadly virus had almost found its way into his brain. But although he had lost his sense of smell, his vision was still good.

Smilodon watched intently now, his head high, his ears and eyes just barely above the tops of the tall grass. He stared unblinking as the mastodon and her calf wandered farther out onto the savanna, away from the shelter of the hammock.

The old cow moved slowly, gently nudging her calf ahead with her trunk, teaching it to browse on the succulent buds of the scattered hackberry bushes. As she fed, she made continuous grumbling sounds deep in her throat, sounds of contentment. She was at ease, unhurried, completely unaware of danger.

Crouching low, Smilodon made a wide circle, creeping up behind them to cut off any possible escape to the nearby hammock. Patiently he watched and waited, his eyes fastened on the little calf.

The cow browsed from bush to bush, and the calf hobbled along beside her, gurgling and sniffing. In imitation of its mother, it twisted and poked its little trunk in and out of the tangle of branches.

Each time the mastodons stopped Smilodon crept closer. He slid on his belly like a small cat stalking a bird, putting out one paw at a time, halting, then going on. A tawny shadow, he flowed through the yellow growth barely rippling the grass.

Lulled by the warm sun, Long Tusk led her calf farther out onto the savanna. She was showing the calf the best sprays of buds and leaves, teaching by example, still unaware of the approaching danger.

Smilodon moved ahead steadily, slowly. His yellow eyes, unblinking, fixed on the calf. The breeze picked up a little. Now the cat could take advantage of the rustling wind and move with less caution. Closer and closer he came, until he was within striking distance—the cow and her calf could not get away. He settled down in the grass, blended into it, then gathered his legs beneath him. His muscles tightened, ready to spring. A deerfly buzzed around his head and landed on his ear. The big cat never twitched.

Suddenly the breeze shifted and the feline scent drifted downwind. The mastodon cow picked it up.

Her tiny eyes did not see the danger but her keen sense of smell told her the cat was near. She spun around to face her enemy, her trunk fully extended to detect the direction. Instantly she knew what it was. She coiled her trunk up under her chin and waited, her long white tusks ready to meet the challenge.

Smilodon too knew the time for concealment was past. He pushed himself to his feet. Like a steel spring he exploded, and headed directly for the calf. In one sweeping motion the cow pushed her young one behind her with her trunk and turned to face the oncoming cat. Her eyes blazed with hate and her sturdy legs and shoulder muscles stood out like unmovable gray boulders.

Smilodon growled deep in his throat. With half-closed eyes, he plunged through the tall grass. He broke through the cover but at that instant he saw he had made a mistake. The cow was standing firm, waiting for him. Quickly he swerved and dodged, trying to get past the long sharp tusks. He overshot his mark and tumbled to one side. He recovered quickly and came back growling, but everywhere he turned, the sharp tusks were there to confront him. Smilodon circled around again and again, first from one side, then from the other. Always the mastodon cow turned with him, keeping her calf safely behind her.

The afternoon sun was beating down now and the big cat stood in the center of the trampled grass panting heavily. He had not expected this. He rushed in repeatedly, trying to cut out the calf. But the cow was wise. She swung around to face him, jabbing, lashing out with her trunk. Once, twice, Smilodon felt the searing hot pain as her sharp tusks raked the flesh of his shoulder.

Still they circled each other, the cow cleverly maneuvering to protect her calf. The big cat tried to get around her. He dashed from one side to the other. But it was no use—she was slowly wearing him down.

Weary of the battle Smilodon backed away, blood streaming from his new wounds. He stood a safe distance away with drooping head, his tongue lolling, trying to catch his breath. But pangs of hunger stabbed through his gut, so he would try once more. He crept through the grass, to come up from behind again; this time he would catch the cow off balance.

But his plan didn't work. The mastodon cow swung around and caught him in midair as he sprang for the calf. In a fit of fury she flung him to the ground. Smilodon rolled over and over, then lay still, panting and out of breath.

Now the cow became careless. Half blind with rage, she rushed for the injured cat to trample him into the dirt, leaving her calf unprotected. Smilodon saw her coming. He saw the calf standing alone, petrified with fear, unable to move.

In that instant Smilodon knew the cow had made a mistake. He waited until she was almost upon him, then leaped to his feet. He dodged to one side as her momentum carried her forward. In three great bounds Smilodon was beside the calf. Wildly he flung himself on the little one's back, then opened his jaws to their full extent and slashed downward, sinking his long saber fangs deep into the tender flesh behind the calf's head. It took only a moment for the big cat to sever a vital artery deep in the little one's neck. This was all he needed. Smilodon jumped to the ground, exhausted, and slunk away into the tall grass.

The cow stormed after him but he stayed well ahead of her. His work done, he holed up under the tangled roots of a nearby strangler fig and waited for the little calf to die. Then he would return for his meal.

For a while the calf stood there squealing, blood streaming down its back and chest. The cow caressed it with her trunk, trying to give comfort. She nudged it gently, pushing the calf's shoulder with her head, urging it toward the safety of the trees. But the trees were still far away and the little animal was growing weak. It hobbled along slowly, weaving back and forth on stubby legs. Then it stumbled and fell to its knees, squealing in panic.

Long Tusk prodded the calf with her trunk as it struggled to get up. But once up, the calf staggered and wobbled, spreading out its legs to keep its balance. Then the little trunk went limp, and the legs buckled. The calf squealed again and sank to its knees in a spattered pool of its own blood. A few moments later it rolled over on its side and lay still.

Long Tusk ran about, trampling the grass in a frenzy of grief. She lifted her trunk high, trumpeted loudly and looked around for an enemy that had long since disappeared. She returned to her calf and touched it gently with her trunk. Desperately she tried to lift it to its feet again, but the little animal did not move.

Again and again the cow came back, hovering over the still body. She nudged it with her foot as if to roll it over. She pulled at its ear, ran the tip of her trunk around its eye and poked it into the little one's mouth, unable to understand why the calf would not get up.

Even as the afternoon wore on, the mother mastodon did not leave. Long after the calf had ceased to breathe she stayed close by. In her agony of sorrow she emitted low trumpeting calls. Three times she started to walk away and three times she returned to caress the little calf with her trunk. Finally, just as the sun swung low, she gave one last trumpeting cry and slowly walked away into the distant hammock of trees leaving her little one alone, lying motionless in the bloodstained grass.

It was what Smilodon had been waiting for. Old and throbbing with pain, he pulled himself to his feet. He could not hunt anymore. He had killed his last mastodon. From now on he would have to seek easier game or become a lowly scavenger. He limped over to the carcass and slashed it down the belly with his great fangs. Then he closed his eyes and pushed his snout into the still warm viscera. With thick slobbering sounds he began to feed, pulling and tugging at the soft gut meat.

But Smilodon could not eat as he used to, gorging

himself until his belly hung. Instead he ate what he could. Then he walked away into the night, past the camp of the clan people and down to the river. There he would lie, in the canebrake, to digest his meal and lick his wounds.

TWENTY-TWO ·

FROM THE TOP OF THE TALL PALM tree Thorn had witnessed the entire battle.

He climbed down slowly and stood near Oom, who
was on his feet now, shaking his head. The
flintmaker had seen some of the struggle over the
tops of the tall grasses; he had guessed the rest. He
cursed under his breath. "Now the ghost walks
again," he said. He picked up his great spear, rolled
up the tan pelt and tucked it under his arm. Then,
stooped over, he limped back to camp.

Thorn stood alone, still thinking about the savage
battle he had just witnessed. He looked out over the
savanna and saw a row of black stormclouds gathering overhead. Jagged flashes of lightning lit up the
dark sky, and thunder crashed. Then came the rain.
It swept over him like a gray curtain, and he stood
and let the drenching torrent engulf him. Water
splashed over his head and shoulders and ran down

his back and legs; it trickled down his face and he put out his tongue and licked his lips. It tasted good and cool and clean.

The rain lasted but a few moments. As fast as it came, it disappeared, and left the western sky tinged with red.

Thorn knew that tonight the coyotes and dire wolves would find the remains of the mastodon calf. In the morning the sun would come up and fill the savanna with a golden glow of warmth. The earth would smell damp, rich with moisture. Great puffs of white clouds would form and float slowly across the blue sky.

Whatever remained of the small, still body of the little mastodon would be torn and scattered across the grasslands. Tomorrow would be a good day for the vultures.

TWENTY-THREE ·

THREE DAYS LATER SMILODON came out of the canebrake. A fever of rage gripped him. He staggered
slightly as he approached the camp where the
dreaded night fires blazed. Undaunted, he walked
past them and stalked boldly around the huts. In one
of them a young girl slept near the entrance. Silently
Smilodon pounced and grabbed her in his jaws.

She died instantly as the long fangs pierced her
neck and severed her spinal cord. They found her
half-eaten body the next morning out on the grasslands, not far from camp. It was Ute, Oom's sister.

The clan people were terrified. They swarmed into
the clearing and milled about in panic in front of
Dour's hut. The old shaman hobbled out wearing his
mourning robe of black jaguar hide. A thin mask of
red clay covered his face, and long strings of blue
and yellow snail shells hung about his neck.

Two men rolled up a heavy palm log for him to stand on.

The elders sat on the hard-packed sand in a tight circle around the shaman. Four hunters stood to one side. Oom strode restlessly up and down, his dark eyes staring wildly, his hands opening and closing with rage. Thorn stood in the background with the women and children, under the shade of the fringe trees.

For a long moment Dour stared at the people. He looked into the terror-stricken faces as if searching for an answer to this terrible scourge. In his shrill, high-pitched voice he began to speak. "Last night we lost a clan sister to the evil cat, Smilodon. The cat is beyond fear. Not the spears, not the flames, not even the smell of fire stop him. We are not safe in our own huts."

A young woman with a child in her arms stood up and cried, "Even during the day we can no longer go out into the fields to dig roots or gather fruit and nuts."

Dour nodded in agreement. "We must find a way to rid our land of this curse." He shook his head gravely. "We have only four hunters. Even if each carried ten spears it would still not be enough to kill the ghostly beast."

A mumbled groan passed through the crowd of clan people.

Dour waited for it to die down. Then he held up his scrawny arms and called out, "But last night I had a vision. I saw Smilodon prowling around the night fires. He turned and looked at me, and his face became that of a girl dressed in otter skins, with dark eyes and long hair. She growls like a cat and strikes out with clawed fingers."

Oom turned quickly, his young face distorted with hate. His bad arm hung down as he limped forward in front of the people. He shook his left fist high over his head. "Kill her!" he shouted. "Kill her the way she killed Ute!" His eyes blazed and tears wet his cheeks. "The spirit girl"—he spit out the words—"sister of evil. Kill her!" he wailed.

One of the elders stood up and shouted, "Aye, she is the demon of terror! Ghost of Smilodon!"

The shaman nodded again and blinked in the bright sunlight, his clay mask cracked and peeling. "It is true," he said, almost softly, "the girl is a changeling. She and the evil cat are one."

Oom spun around. "Why do we stand here?" he snarled. "Let us be at it before she kills again."

The elders rose up. The people shouted in a frenzy of fear, "Death to Smilodon!" The chant carried out over the clearing. "Death to the spirit girl!"

Dour's thin lips drew back in a satisfied sneer. "Then let it be so." He held up a knotted hand. "But remember, she runs like a deer, she climbs like an ocelot. To get close enough to put a spear through her heart will not be easy."

Oom stalked back and forth, restless, impatient to be off. He lifted his good arm and pointed toward the forest. "Then we will lay snares and set vine traps and deadfalls along all the trails. We will carry extra spears and knives, and hunt her down day after day, until we are rid of her."

The clan people rose up again, chanting, "Death to the spirit girl! Death to the changeling!"

Thorn stood in the shadows. He gritted his teeth to hold back the words of protest that were on his lips. Filled with hate and fear of the evil cat, the people were turning their anger on the one person they could not understand.

The hunters returned to their huts and came back with knives and cutting stones. They brought coils of vine and long strips of bark rope. Each hunter carried three long, slender flint-tipped spears. With vengeful oaths they raised their weapons overhead, then followed Oom as he limped slowly out across the clearing and into the forest.

Thorn watched them go. His eyes narrowed and he shook his head. They search for an innocent girl, he thought. It is as though they were going out to track down a vicious beast. Quietly he backed into the shadows of the fringe trees and crept out of camp. The sandy earth muffled the sound of his footsteps as he made his way through the loblolly pines.

When he reached the river he glanced around quickly, then followed the winding bank until he came to the shallows. He looked up into the overhanging branches of the gum trees and called softly, "Fonn." He waded out into the stream and called again. "Fonn." There was no answer.

He hurried down to the place where they had fished together only a few days before. She was not there either. He hurried alongside the river, calling her name again and again. The morning passed without an answer.

Then, early in the afternoon, at a bend in the river where the waters ran slow, he heard her laugh. He stooped under the low-hanging branches of the dahoon trees to get closer, and peered through the leaves. There he saw her in a quiet backwater pool, swimming with a school of manatees.

He smiled as he watched her playing underwater with the plump gray animals. They rolled over and around her. Their heads popped up beside her like those of fat, bewhiskered old men. She scratched their bristly snouts and fed them handfuls of water lettuce. One of the docile animals floated on its back holding a baby in its arms.

He had almost forgotten why he was here, when Shadow swooped down shouting his loud *ca-ha*.

Fonn looked up quickly. She saw Thorn and waved. Tiny freckles of pale green duckweed clung to her bare arms and shoulders. She laughed. "Come in, clan boy. The manatees will teach you how to swim. We play like brothers and sisters."

Thorn shook his head vigorously and burst out, "No, there is no time."

The girl pulled herself out of the pool. She came toward him frowning. Her otterskin breechcloth dripped with water. "What is the matter?"

"Smilodon has killed Ute, clan sister of Oom."

"What? When?"

"Last night, right through the fires."

For a long moment the girl stared off into the distance. Her eyes narrowed. "Something is very wrong. The old cat acts strangely."

"The people say it is your doing. Even now the hunters search for you with spears and ropes. They are angry and"—he looked up at her—"they talk of killing."

"How many hunters?"

"Four. Oom is with them."

The girl frowned. "Oom too?"

"Yes, he is like a bear, mad with sorrow. He calls you the ghost of Smilodon."

Fonn pushed strings of wet hair out of her eyes. "I am sorry for Oom. But now he too is dangerous. I must think of something to do."

"Go back to the grotto," said Thorn. "They will not follow you there."

The girl thought for a while, biting her lower lip. Then she said, "You are right. The saber cat runs amok. Even Great Claw is not safe here. Tomorrow I will go down to the wallow and lead him back to my country."

Just then Shadow began flying about, flapping his wings with excitement, shouting his warning.

Thorn glanced around and peered through the trees.

"They come," said Fonn. "Go, before they find us." As he turned to leave she put her hand on his arm. "Clan boy, you are still a good friend."

Thorn trudged back to camp, taking a roundabout way through the loblolly pines in order to avoid the hunters. All afternoon he waited in Nema's hut.

Nema rocked back and forth as she sat by the cook fire chewing on her ague twig. "Now the cat is bold, he fears nothing."

Thorn shrugged. "The girl is not to blame for that."

"I am an old woman," said Nema, "but I know this: Smilodon is different. He was not here before the girl came. Maybe she holds a power over him that we do not understand. If this is so, then she is also to blame for the killing."

The boy was sure this was not true. But he held his tongue.

The sun went down and the shadows of the cabbage palms fell across the clearing. Thorn heard the hunters come back. He ran outside and saw Oom limping into the clearing. He ran up to him, bursting to know. "Did—did you find her?"

The young flintmaker glared at him, his jaw tight, as if he did not know him. "We did not," he said. "But we set our traps, and we will go out again tomorrow and every day until we get her."

Thorn sighed deeply and walked back to his hut. Fonn was still safe.

· TWENTY-FOUR

DARKNESS CAME AND THE NIGHT fires blazed high, ringing the little camp in a bright yellow glow. Thorn helped the clan people gather brush and dry timbers, piling them high to build a double ring of fires for extra protection against the prowling cat. Showers of sparks flew up into the dark sky as the heavy logs were thrown onto the flames.

Later Thorn returned to the hut. Nema was already sleeping, stretched out on her llama-skin pelt. Thorn lay near the entrance, where he could look out and see the night sky full of stars. He lay with his hands behind his head, thinking about Fonn. He smelled the burning pine wood, and was thankful for the double ring of fires that encircled the camp.

Then his eyes grew heavy and he fell asleep. How long he slept he did not know, but he was awakened by a cry, a deep cry of pain. He jumped up and peered into the darkness. The cry came again, louder this time, from somewhere near the center of the camp.

Thorn dashed into the clearing and glanced around the huts sleepily as the clan people came streaming out. He stood there for a moment, startled. Then he saw Smilodon in the light of the fires. The big cat held a man in his jaws by the back of the neck. He dropped the man and glared at Thorn. His lips curled and he snarled. His long white fangs flashed in the firelight. He staggered for a moment, then grabbed the man by one arm and pulled him across the clearing, out of the light.

Thorn stood dumbfounded as the cat disappeared into the darkness. He walked out toward the edge of the clearing and saw the groove marks in the sand where the man had been dragged. As the clan people moved about in panic, Thorn ran back into his hut and picked up his spear. Then he raced across the clearing to wake Oom. The young flintmaker was not in his hut; the interior was a shambles. Bloodstains covered the floor. The big skull lay dumped over on its side, an ocelot headband hung from one of the long fangs. Flint spearheads and stone tools lay scattered everywhere.

Thorn shook his head. A cold chill crept through his body. Oom! The man he had seen in Smilodon's jaws was Oom. Without thinking Thorn raced into the clearing again and immediately picked out a flaming torch from the fire.

In the rush of people he bumped into Nema. She grabbed him by the arm, her eyes wide, glinting in the firelight. "Where are you going?"

He pulled away from her and said nothing.

Nema screamed after him, "No, Thorn, no! There is nothing you can do!"

But he did not hear. He raced off into the darkness with two of the clan hunters close behind him. Holding their torches high, they picked up the blood spoor and followed it across the scrublands and through the pines. It led in a wide circle down to the river, and there they saw the marks of a man's heels dragged along the sandy bank.

Filled with a burning rage, the boy followed the trail of blood and bits of torn pelt from Oom's apron. The other two hunters came pounding after him, trying to keep up. Thorn followed the drag marks in the sand until they veered into a thick forest of gum trees. There they ended. Hanging roots, dangling vines and lianas climbed and looped in and around the trunks of the tall trees, creating a dark maze of tangled vegetation.

Thorn gritted his teeth and forced his way between the trees, holding his torch in one hand, his spear in the other. He struggled desperately over the protruding roots, and squeezed deeper and deeper through the tangle of forest, elbowing his way around the trees and looping vines.

The two other hunters stopped. "It is no good, boy," one called after him. "Smilodon is waiting. The thickets are dark—no room to throw the spears."

Thorn turned. "Wait, then," he said. He could barely see them in the dim light. "I am going on."

Driven by a blind hatred, the boy fought his way through the mass of twisted vines. Hacking at them with his spear, shoving others aside. But the trail was growing faint. The blood spoor was played out. Yet here and there fern and palmetto stems were trampled into the earth plainly enough to follow. With his head down Thorn shouldered his way in. Low-growing saplings whipped across his chest. Then he ran into a tough web of silk. He dropped his spear and tore at the web, ripping it away from his arms and shoulders. At the same time he felt the prickles of a huge spider running across his face.

Darkness faded as the first light of dawn washed across the eastern sky. Exhausted as he was, Thorn refused to give up. He wormed his way deeper into the forest, not even sure where he was.

His torch had gone out, so he threw it aside; its embers sizzled in the damp earth. Now all around him the birds began to wake up. Fork-tailed fly-catchers filled the dawn with their long whistling calls. Mangrove cuckoos rang through the treetops with their deep-throated *cowk-cowk*. Normally Thorn would have reveled in this jubilant chorus, but this morning he did not even notice it.

Then he heard a low, deep-throated growl. It came from directly in front of him and he knew it was Smilodon. Thorn stopped and lifted his spear even though he knew it would do little good. He waited and listened, then started forward again, cautiously making his way around the boles of the towering gum trees. In the morning light he could see only some few birds and the dappled gray wall of lianas and vines.

Yet Thorn knew Smilodon lay in the underbrush not far away, waiting. He heard the crack of twigs and the rustle of dried palm leaves. He stood quietly and held his breath. Then he crept ahead slowly, peering through the mass of leaves and vines. The stench of cat was heavy in his nostrils, and he knew he was getting close. He leaned forward, staring into the trampled brush.

The cat was gone. But there on the forest floor lay Oom's blood-smeared body. Thorn rushed over to him, leaned down and touched the man's cheek. It was cold and lifeless. The man stared at the sky, his eyes glazed with a dull gray mist. His lips were white. A trickle of blood ran down from the corner of his mouth.

Thorn turned away, sick to his stomach. He could not look at the open belly wounds where the cat had been feeding. He covered his face with his hands and sat down beside the dead man. Maybe Oom had been right, Thorn thought; maybe Smilodon is an evil spirit come back to seek revenge. Maybe the girl is a changeling. Tears welled up in his eyes. He shook his head and wiped them away with the back of his hand. No, it was not true.

Slowly Thorn got to his feet. In a fit of rage he threw his spear aside. He reached down and lifted Oom under the arms and dragged him backward through the woods. The man was heavy. The boy strained and pulled, jostling the body around the fat tree trunks. Sharp thorns slapped against the back of his arms and legs and left long red welts as he shouldered his way through the tangle of forest. Sweat trickled down his forehead and deerflies buzzed around his nose and into the damp corners of his eyes. He did not even notice.

The eastern sky was awash in light as the boy dragged Oom out of the gum forest. The two hunters met Thorn at the edge of the scrub. They lashed the dead man between two poles and carried him into camp just as they had done with Thorn's father four summers before.

They placed Oom gently on the ground in the center of the clearing. The clan people gathered around as women prepared the body. They smeared it with yellow clay and sprinkled it with wood ash, then wrapped it in palm leaves.

In the afternoon Dour came out of his hut. He wore his black jaguar skin and his woodpecker headdress. He led the procession as clanspeople carried the body on a rack of branches into the scrub. There the women dug a deep hole in the sand with large turtle-shell scoops. They lowered Oom to the bottom of the hole, then filled it with sand. Finally, heavy palm logs were laid on top of the grave to protect it from scavenging dire wolves and armadillos.

Thorn stayed behind after the brief ceremony was over. He stared down at the fresh palm leaves and water lilies decorating the grave. As he stood there he heard someone come up behind him: it was Dour with his pot of smoldering titi leaves.

The shaman leaned toward him. "Now you know the girl is truly a changeling." The old man put a bony hand on his shoulder. "You are the one who must kill her."

The boy cringed. He was bitter, full of vengeance, but he did not want to kill.

"Go to Oom's hut," said the old man. "There you will see what your evil friend has done."

TWENTY-FIVE ·

NUMB WITH GRIEF, THORN WALKED across the clearing to the flintmaker's hut. He looked around the dim interior for a moment, and smelled the earthy odor of flint chips, and bone shavings on the floor. With a weary sigh he gathered up the scattered hand tools and bone hammers. He turned over the big skull and set it back in its proper place.

He picked up the stone hammer the flintmaker had used to make the great spear. His fingers curled around it and he thought of the many times he had sat here while Oom carved out a flint ax or a knife. Then he moved about glumly, putting things back in order, piling the ivory tusks and the flint cores into neat stacks the way Oom always kept them.

At the rear of the hut he stooped over to pick up a broken conch shell and saw the moleskin pouch lying at his feet. He took it and unrolled it, exposing the delicate willow-leaf spearhead within the hide.

He placed it gingerly on top of the skull, then pulled his hand back as if he were touching something evil.

Now he reached for a small core of flint. He felt the cold, hard smoothness of it in the palm of his hand, and more memories came flooding back, memories of summers past when Oom had listened to his stories while he worked over his flints. Thorn shook his head and tried to drive the thoughts from his mind. In a fit of temper, he threw the flint to the ground and kicked at the big skull.

The shaman came in and stood near the entrance of the hut, his tiny eyes taking in the scene. "Good," he said, "you are angry with the girl. It will make it easier."

Thorn spun around. He stared at this wrinkled little man standing before him in the shadows. "Not at the girl," he said curtly. "At myself. Oom tried to tell me, but I did not listen."

"Ah, so now you know she is the evil one."

"I—I do not think that is true."

"Why?"

"Because she is my friend."

"So Smilodon is also your friend."

"Never! I hate the evil cat."

"Then you must also hate the girl, for she and Smilodon are one and the same."

Thorn looked up, the pain and agony of the terrible decision contorting his face. He shook his head violently, his hair flying about his shoulders. "Then let the hunters kill her," he said. "She is not their friend. They will not care."

The shaman scowled. "You know as I do, she will run from the hunters. They will never catch her. You are the only one who can get close enough to do it."

Thorn knew the old shaman was right. He was the only one the girl trusted.

"Remember," said Dour. "The omen is not yet fulfilled." He waited, watching the boy's face, then added, "Nema is next."

Thorn winced. He spoke slowly, almost in a whisper. "I must kill the girl to save Nema?"

"It is the only way," said the shaman. He leaned over and tapped his finger on the willow-leaf spearhead. "Here is your weapon. It will fly straight and true, and pierce the heart of the evil spirit. It cannot miss."

The boy was silent for a while, mulling the shaman's words over in his head. Then slowly the glint of a plan came into his mind. "Kill any evil spirit?"

"Any," said Dour. "Without fail."

Thorn picked up the amber-yellow spearhead. His hand trembled as he turned it over in his fingers. He felt the keen sharpness of it but this time he was careful not to cut his thumb. His jaw tightened in determination, and he laid the spearhead on the big skull. "I will do it," he said as he stood up.

Dour drew in his breath. He turned to leave, then stopped. "It must be done before nightfall, or the changeling will kill again."

Thorn's hands shook. He feared what was about to happen.

After the shaman left, Thorn selected a thin ironwood pole from a stack at the rear of the hut. With a flint knife he scraped away the layer of bark until he had a long slender shaft taller than himself. Next he split one end. Into this he carefully wedged the delicate willow-leaf spearhead.

He worked quickly, remembering how Oom had made his spears. He searched through the leather sacks lying around the hut until he found what he wanted, a ball of dried catgut. This he soaked in a turtle shell full of warm water. When it was soft and pliable he wound it carefully around the base of the spearhead and bound it tightly to the shaft. Finally he dried the spear over a small hearth fire to make the catgut hard and strong.

Now the spear was ready. It was straight and strong. Thorn stepped into the clearing and held it over his head. The spearhead flashed in the bright sunshine. "Now," he said, "the omen will be fulfilled."

At that moment the great cat roared. The thundering sound seemed to come from all sides, the river, the savanna, the oak wood.

Thorn gritted his teeth and breathed deeply. With the magic spear in his hand and a spear thrower tucked under his belt, he started for the river. He carried a leather pouch full of dried meat and fruit, and he talked to himself to keep up his courage. "It will be as easy as spearing a garfish or a river hog," he said under his breath. He said it with a bravado he did not really feel, but he said it anyway.

The sun was high and a steamy haze hung over

the river as Thorn made his way. His heart pounded in him. Black rails and coots ran ahead of him along the sandy shore. A line of skimmers flew low over the water, their long bills leaving V-shaped ripples in the mirrorlike surface.

Thorn plunged on. He held his head down and looked for prints in the damp sand, but he found none. He headed into the scrub. A flock of ground doves flew up at his approach and a big gopher turtle plodded out of his way.

But none of these things caught his eye. The one Thorn was looking for was not there. He made his way into the oak wood. Here the big trees spread out in endless rows, the tips of their branches touching, like huge gray ghosts holding hands. Long strands of curly moss hung down from the outstretched limbs. Thorn crept silently under the living draperies, studying the ground for marks and broken twigs. Again he found none.

Then, just ahead, something moved in the shadows. Thorn heard the rustle of leaves. A flash of brown hide caught his eye. With trembling fingers he placed his spear into the notch of his thrower. Slowly he raised it.

The holly branches before him parted, and a big white-tailed deer stepped onto the path. It spun around, its black nose twitching. For a moment it froze in place. Then it turned and disappeared into the underbrush.

Thorn lowered his spear. He waited until the pounding in his chest had stopped, then went on.

The sun was high when he headed toward the open savanna. The rays slanted down turning the grass into waves of burnished gold that stretched far into the distance. In the west Thorn made out a gathering of vultures, tiny black spots soaring high in the sky, circling lazily over the wallow.

Just in front of him sleek silver hawks with black wings and split tails soared low, searching for skinks and rat snakes; not far away, a group of brush pigs rooted noisily beneath a stand of gumbo trees.

Thorn pushed his way through the waist-high grass, going deeper and deeper into the savanna. A herd of longhorn bison thundered off ahead of him. He waited until the sound died away, then he walked on, the dry grass crunching under his feet. He studied the horizon. Everything seemed peaceful and quiet.

All at once a flock of gray red-capped cranes rose out of the grass. They flapped up in fright, trumpeting loudly—*karoo, karoo.* Then in ponderous, labored strokes, they flew off toward the west.

The boy stopped. He gripped his spear tightly and stared ahead. Not far off, he could see a long, tawny shape slinking through the meadow. It disappeared for a moment. He heard a movement in the grass. The beast was coming toward him.

Thorn planted his feet wide apart and braced himself, holding his spear up. The rustling sound came closer. He waited, his eyes staring at the moving curtain of grass. He heard his pulse pounding in his ears and felt a giddiness in the pit of his stomach. The rustling sound stopped, then started again. Thorn held his breath. He drew his arm back ready to throw.

With a low growl the beast broke out of cover. It was a young puma hunting for swamp deer. It looked at Thorn in surprise, then snarled and bounded away across the savanna.

Thorn let out a deep sigh and lowered his spear, then he started out again pushing deeper into the waist-high grass. High overhead, he saw a big condor. It circled slowly in the warm afternoon sun but seemed to glide lower and lower. Thorn walked on, watching the big bird yet trying to keep a lookout on the grasslands ahead.

Then his heart leaped as a huge head suddenly reared up over the top of the waving grass. The boy gasped. It was Smilodon. The great shaggy head swayed from side to side. Two long brown-stained fangs jutted down from either side of the upper jaw. The yellow eyes with their dark pupils stared at the boy, so close he could see the watery fluid running down the cheeks from the corner of each eye.

Thorn gripped his spear tightly. His hands shook. "Come, evil spirit," he mumbled. "I have been looking for you. Come closer. Let the magic spear pierce your heart."

The cat crept forward slowly. With each step he seemed to grow larger. Thorn stood firm. His hands trembled as he raised his spear and hooked it into the notch of the spear thrower. He brought his arm back, ready to throw. At that moment the cat disappeared.

The boy waited. He looked around cautiously. Off

to one side he saw the grass move. The cat was circling to come up behind him. Thorn waited again, listening, watching.

Once again Smilodon rose up above the tall grass. His head still swung from side to side and he breathed heavily. He seemed crazed and confused. He blinked in the bright sunshine, long strings of white froth hanging from his black lips. His lower jaw dropped open and he growled a deep gurgling sound.

Thorn drew back his arm as far as he could; he held the thrower in his right hand and aimed with his left. The great head, the broad chest and shoulders were in plain view.

Thorn mumbled, "The omen is done." With a powerful thrust he hurled the spear, aiming for the heart. The weapon flew through the air with tremendous force and struck the beast full in the chest. The fragile point shattered against the tough hide. The long shaft broke in two and fell at Smilodon's feet.

Thorn's mouth dropped open. In that instant he knew the cat was no spirit—Smilodon was flesh and blood.

But now was not the time to think. The big cat was coming toward him. Thorn jammed his spear thrower under his belt and ran. As he plunged through the tall grass, he could hear the cat crashing close behind him. Thorn ran with his head down, not daring to look back. He expected sharp claws to pull him down any moment.

Then suddenly he realized the thrashing sounds

had stopped. He turned and looked around. The cat was gone. The boy stood still, trying to control the shaking in his legs. *Where was the cat?*

Once more Smilodon rose out of the tall grass, this time off to one side, closer to Thorn than before. The boy jumped back, startled. He ran, his breath rasping in his throat, and he felt a tiredness creep into his legs. But his feet pounded as he forced himself to go on.

He came to a narrow stream that wound through the grasslands in sweeping curves. He teetered on the edge of the bank, then jumped and landed with a splash knee-deep in the murky waters. Quickly he waded to the other bank and started to climb up, but tired in every muscle, he fell back. He lay there for a moment, gasping for air. Rivulets of sweat poured down his face and into his eyes, blinding him. He wiped them away with the back of his hand. When he glanced back over his shoulder, he could see Smilodon crouched on the opposite side, snarling, ready to spring.

· TWENTY-SIX

THORN REACHED UP, SEARCHING for a handhold in the muddy bank. Again and again he tried, grasping at the wet weeds, slipping and sliding in the mud—and still expecting Smilodon to pounce at any moment. Then, over the growl of the cat, he heard the familiar *ca-ha, ca-ha* of Shadow. He shook his head to clear his brain, certain that it was only his imagination. But a moment later Shadow flew down and landed on his shoulder. The crow squawked loudly in his ear and Thorn saw the sunlight reflected in the bird's ebony eyes. Shadow flapped away, then returned, circling, cawing.

Thorn wondered where Shadow had come from. And how the bird had found him?

Once again Shadow swooped up through the slanting rays of sunlight. He hovered, then came down, his wings brushing against the boy's face.

Suddenly Thorn remembered the girl—she had said she would come to the wallow to get Great

Claw. The bird was calling Thorn to follow.

Desperately the boy groped and clawed at the muddy bank, each time sliding back into the water. But this time he felt the roughness of a protruding root and his fingers closed around it. He pulled with all his strength and very slowly hauled himself out onto the bank. He lay there panting, exhausted, and glanced back across the creek. The big cat was still there, his yellow, bloodshot eyes boring into him.

Thorn stared back as if in a trance. Why did the cat not spring? The stream was not deep; with a few steps Smilodon could splash across. Instead he crouched on his belly, snarling, his head weaving back and forth, unsteady. He reached out a front paw and touched the edge of the creek, then quickly pulled back, as if the water were hot. He snarled again and thick strings of saliva dripped from his jaws. He shied away from the water as if sick, or blind. The cat stood up and staggered, then turned and walked upstream along the bank.

Shadow kept up his persistent call, flying off then coming back. Something was wrong. Slowly Thorn got to his feet, his eyes still searching the bank where the cat had been. Then he limped through the tall grass toward the wallow. For now he seemed to be safe.

At first he walked as if in his sleep. His breath burning in his throat, he stumbled headlong through the grass, trying to follow the erratic bird. Then, in a hazy blur, he saw the tall palm trees of the hammock, and the wallow just in front of it.

He stopped to rest. With legs spread apart he

leaned over, breathing hard. If he could just rest for a short while, he would be all right. But the crow came back, nagging and scolding him harshly. "All right," Thorn gasped, "I am coming, I am coming." He heard a rustling in the grass. Out of the corner of his eye he saw the big cat. Smilodon had jumped the creek at a narrow spot farther upstream and was now cutting across in front of him.

The boy groaned. He hunched down in the tall grass to hide and to think. There was only one thing to do. He had to run, he had to get past the cat. If he could reach the trees behind the wallow he would be safe. There was a chance—the cat seemed muddled. Thorn pulled the spear thrower from his belt. He lifted it high and threw it as far as he could off to one side.

The cat heard it fall and went after it.

Thorn took a deep breath and started running, plunging through the tall grass. He tripped and fell, but picked himself up.

Breathlessly he raced on. He did not look back, but he could hear the thrashing sounds of the beast close behind him in the grass. Thorn's legs felt like stones, and each step was more painful than the one before. The hammock of palms loomed up ahead of him. Grunting and panting he forced himself on.

Then, over the sound of his pounding feet, he heard a cry: "Clan boy!" He peered through the trickles of sweat that ran down his face. In a haze he saw Fonn standing near the edge of the wallow, and right behind her the giant sloth. He knew now she was no changeling.

He tried to warn her, but the words caught in his throat. He stumbled toward the palms, the cat panting and wheezing right behind him. Now she saw. Fonn stood frozen to the spot.

"Run," he gasped, "run for the trees." He reached Fonn and pulled her by one arm toward the hammock. His legs gave out and he fell, pulling her down with him. They tumbled over each other. Fonn jumped to her feet but Thorn lay still, gasping for breath, unable to move. The moments passed. He caught his breath and sat up, holding his heaving sides. He looked back and shook his head, unable to believe what he saw.

Smilodon had not followed. Instead the big cat crouched in the grass, slinking forward on his belly, staring up at the giant sloth. The deadly rabies virus had reached the cat's brain. He could smell nothing. He could see only shapes and movement. Now Great Claw loomed up in front of him, the largest image in his fading field of vision.

Smilodon weaved back and forth. He dropped his lower jaw, opening his mouth wide, freeing his long saber fangs. With a deep guttural growl, he charged. He leaped high and slashed with his sharp fangs at Great Claw's chest. But the fangs did not penetrate the thick hide.

The sloth moaned in anger and stumbled backward into the wallow. Supported by his massive tail, he raked his attacker with deadly claws and slashed long flesh wounds across the big cat's flank and shoulders. Blood flowed freely, and soon the tawny pelt was smeared with wide stains of bright red.

Spellbound by the savage struggle, Thorn and Fonn looked on from the other side of the wallow.

"The cat is mad," Fonn said. "Never would a saber cat attack a full-grown sloth from the front."

Again and again Smilodon rushed in stabbing and slashing. Each time Great Claw was knocked backward by the force of the mad rush; each time he stumbled deeper into the oozing sand. Yet the clumsy beast would not give up. Moaning in rage, he lashed out with his long black claws, leaving streaks of crimson across the great cat's body.

Back and forth they fought, roaring and growling, churning up the wallow until it was stained red with blood. Great Claw lashed out with his tail. It struck the big cat full across the chest and sent him rolling into the wet sand.

The giant sloth braced himself for the next rush, but the big cat lay still, his chest heaving rapidly. Great Claw moaned in anger and turned, trying to pull himself out of the sinking mire. In that moment Smilodon saw his chance. He got to his feet and limped painfully toward the wallow.

Thorn saw what was about to happen. He held his breath. Fonn gasped.

With a last, mighty effort Smilodon threw himself on Great Claw's back and plunged his long fangs deep into the neck of the clumsy beast. Great Claw tried to shake him off but the big cat hung on, stabbing again and again.

Once more Great Claw stumbled backward. He sank deeper into the wallow in an agony of rage and pain, with Smilodon clinging to his back. The giant sloth twisted and turned and bellowed as he staggered. His life's blood was flowing away like a river from the gaping wounds in his neck. He began to weave in a drunken stupor, then fell headlong into the oozing sands.

Smilodon fell with him. Feebly he struggled to his feet, then stood over his victim. But his head hung low. He too was finished. Weakened by the loss of blood and the virus seething in his brain, he slumped across the fallen sloth, dead. Slowly they sank, until they were half buried in the gurgling sands.

Fonn shook her head and turned away. She looked up at Thorn. "I do not want to see any more."

Together they walked back to the clan camp. When the people heard the news they gathered around Fonn, offering her fruits and nuts. They forgot about the spirits, they forgot about changelings and ghosts. The omen was fulfilled. That was all that mattered. The evil cat was dead.

That night Thorn stood alone staring into the fire. Fonn came up beside him. She spoke quietly. "Will you go back with me to the land of the Lake Dwellers tomorrow?"

"I have thought about it," said Thorn, "but I do not want to leave Nema."

"Perhaps she will go with us," said Fonn.

The boy looked up quickly. "Perhaps."

"I have talked with others who may come later."

Thorn grinned. "Perhaps we will start a new clan," he said.

"Perhaps," Fonn answered.

After Fonn went back to the hut where she was to sleep, Thorn stood by the fire thinking about the next day and the days ahead. He did not hear Dour coming up behind him until the old man spoke. "So now you go to another country?"

The boy nodded.

"Then I will have no one to bring me gifts of fish and snails from the river," said the old man, with a deep sigh.

Thorn looked up, a glint of humor in his eyes. He bowed low. "Ah yes, wise one. I will come back often, with fat fish from the big waters, and shells and crabs as big as your head."

The old man cocked his head to one side. His lips parted slightly. It had been a long time since Thorn had seen him smile.

The next morning some of the clan hunters went out to the wallow to see the fallen giants. They were not alone; the vultures were already there. Some of them waddled across the carcasses and tore greedily at the exposed flesh. Others sat in the dead cypress trees, hunched over like mourners in black feathers waiting their turn at the kill.

Soon the dire wolves arrived. They had seen the circling vultures and now came to claim their share of the feast. Light of foot, they scampered across the wallow to reach the floating bodies.

So too came the fish crows, the gangly storks and

the slinking coyotes. It was a great gathering of scavengers. With fang and claw and bill they ripped and slashed. They pushed and jostled each other. They squabbled and growled and tore off great chunks of meat.

The clan hunters watched in silence and wonder. They had no way of knowing that they were witnessing the passing of the giants, the end of an era.

· EPILOGUE

THEY ROAMED THE PENINSULA for millions of years, these giant beasts—mammoths and mastodons, longhorn bison, shaggy old ground sloths. Then slowly they gave up their domain to new, smaller breeds of animals.

Shorthorn bison spread over the grasslands. Lobo wolves took over the forests and savannas. Smaller, more agile black bears crowded out the lumbering white-faced cave bears.

With no dead mammoths and mastodons to feed on, the giant condors died out, leaving the skies to smaller turkey buzzards and vultures. It was the end of an era, the last of the giants, and Smilodon, sometimes called sabertooth tiger, followed them all into oblivion.

Even Thorn and his fellow Paleo-Indian hunters disappeared, to be replaced by new hunters, men and women from the north who came with bows and arrows, weapons more deadly and accurate than ever before. They brought new practices, such as farming and pottery-making. They spoke new languages. They wore beaded skins, and feathers on their heads. They reigned for thousands of years, until other men and women came from across the sea. With guns and plows the newcomers swarmed into the forests and grasslands and turned them into farms and plantations. They multiplied rapidly, but their rule lasted perhaps barely a few hundred years.

Then a new breed of giants roared down from the north, more powerful and ruthless than any before. These were tractors, earth-movers, steam shovels and bulldozers. These great metallic monsters tore up the earth: the farms and plantations were plowed under, swamps were drained to make way for super-highways, airports, sports arenas, recreation centers and shopping malls. Millions of new people followed the migration. Today they fill the land. How long will they reign? Who can say? But as surely as the sun rises, they will one day follow Thorn and Smilodon into the past—and something new will take their place.